HER FAKE IRISH HUSBAND

MICHELE BROUDER

Editing by Jessica Peirce

Book Cover Design by www.madcatdesigns.net

Her Fake Irish Husband

To God be the Glory.

Chapter One

Rachel Parker breezed through the reception area of Bixby International, coffee cup in hand, and stopped at the desk to have a quick chat with Poppy, the receptionist. Emblazoned in brass on the wood-grain wall behind Poppy was the company name and logo. Every time Rachel read the sign, the website jingle sailed through her head: "Bixby International—no problem too big, no problem too small. We tackle them all."

"How was your weekend?" Rachel asked, leaning over the bar-height counter of the reception area.

Poppy smiled at Rachel. Although she was only a few years younger than Rachel, her life was far more adventurous. And she had the most amazing boyfriend, so unlike the one Rachel had broken up with the year before. Rachel envied her. Hearing her tales of the weekend on Monday mornings was almost as good as reading a book. Almost. Poppy's life was about clubbing and traveling with her boyfriend. Or hanging out with her girlfriends, whereas Rachel's life was more sedate. There was nothing she enjoyed more than settling down with a good book and a large cup of coffee. Throw in some rain and she couldn't dream of anything better. There were also her nieces and a nephew, ranging in age from four to twelve, children of her two older brothers. She was actively involved in their lives. Another indicator of her vicarious life: she was helping to raise another woman's kids. But truth be told, she was content. Somewhat.

"Raymond took me to that new club on Madison," Poppy gushed. She was all curly platinum-blonde hair, ruby-red lips, and eyelash extensions. Sometimes Rachel, with her shoulder-length brown hair, her uniform headband, and minimal makeup, felt positively mousy compared to her younger counterpart. "We went to opening night. I've never drunk so much in my life! There were a lot of fit men there." She winked at Rachel.

"It sounds lovely." Rachel smiled.

Poppy burst out laughing. "Lovely? Lovely is taking your granny to lunch! Come on, Rachel!"

Rachel shrugged, suddenly feeling inadequate. She had never been a popular girl, and she had been okay with that. It was foolish to compare herself with Poppy. And besides, she used to enjoy going to lunch with her Gran.

"Raymond served me breakfast in bed yesterday morning." Poppy smiled. "Went out in the pouring rain and got a couple of magazines I liked and the newspaper for himself and served me a raspberry mimosa with French bread and caviar."

"Caviar?" Rachel repeated. She'd never had caviar in her life.

"Yes, Raymond knows how much I love caviar."

Rachel tried to picture a man running out in the pouring rain for her to procure a newspaper and pastries. She couldn't get the image in proper focus.

"Anyway, after a night of drinking, didn't we get up early Saturday morning and head off to a travel agent?"

Rachel raised her eyebrows. Poppy did things like this: spontaneous and impulsive. Planned trips to the other side of the world at the drop of a hat and ate caviar for breakfast. Whereas Rachel was a planner and an organizer. If she tried to do anything spontaneous without any prep, it would probably kill her. "Where are you jetting off to now?"

"Phuket," Poppy replied.

Rachel's brow wrinkled. "Thailand?"

"The one and only. We're going to a pearl farm!"

Rachel smiled politely, not wanting to ask what a pearl farm was in case she looked stupid. She drew her own conclusions.

"You should go sometime!" Poppy suggested.

Rachel shook her head quickly. "No thanks, that wouldn't be for me." She wasn't even one for crossing state lines, let alone traveling to the other side of the world.

The receptionist laughed. "Oh, that's right, you have a fear of flying."

"Not so much a fear of flying as a fear of crashing," Rachel corrected.

The other girl shrugged. Rachel felt the need to defend her quiet, solitary life and she didn't know why. "I'm perfectly content right where I am."

Poppy rolled her eyes, surprising Rachel. "How can you be? Someday, Rachel, you're going to shrivel up and die from boredom."

Rachel blinked, stung. She knew she'd led a quiet life, but she didn't think it was boring. Well, at least it wasn't to her. But she supposed it might appear that way to some.

Poppy attached her headset and took the phones off the answering service. "Rachel, instead of reading about other people's lives, you need to start living your own."

Rachel protested, "I'm happy with my life."

Poppy raised her eyebrows. "If you say so."

Rachel was about to ask her to join her for lunch but thought the other girl would be bored to tears and so bit back the idea.

"Why does Ben get to do all the traveling for the company?" Poppy asked. "I'd love his job. All that traveling all over the world. Get to go to all those places on the company's dime."

Rachel didn't answer her. It was an arrangement that had suited both her and Ben. She did all of the research and he got out of the office and sometimes, out of the country. It had been like that for almost five years.

Rachel's phone beeped and she looked at it and frowned. "I've been summoned to Mr. Bixby's office."

"Hopefully you're not being fired."

Rachel glanced at her, mortified.

Poppy spoke hurriedly, "No, no, Rachel, I was just teasing you. Of course you won't be getting fired. You've been here so long you're practically an institution around here." *Just throw me my retirement party now*, Rachel thought but said, "Well, I better get going and see what's up."

"Good luck!" Poppy called out after her.

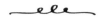

On the walk to her boss's office, Rachel recalled Poppy's words and realized that although there was some truth to them, they still hurt. Her lack of a life was apparently a problem and here she was, a problem solver! Maybe she needed to tackle her own personal life with the same enthusiasm she channeled into tackling the problems that came across her desk.

Pausing outside the office of the owner and CEO of Bixby International, Rachel could hardly imagine what Mr. Bixby could want. She couldn't remember being summoned to his office in the recent past. Hired ten years back with a history degree in hand, she was still as excited about her job as she was the day she'd started. She and Mr. Bixby usually met up once a month in a prearranged meeting to discuss Rachel's current work projects, which could be just about anything.

That's what she loved about her job. Every day was something different, something challenging. Two months earlier, they'd had a client who was seeking an original Imperial Fabergé egg for his wife for her fiftieth birthday. That has been a lot of fun. A year before that, the company had been contacted by a solicitor from Somerset, England, looking for a very distant relative of his deceased client who had left behind a considerable estate. It had taken her six months to track down a fourth cousin and tell them they were in for a windfall. So, yes, she loved her job. And she was good at it.

Taking a deep breath, she knocked tentatively on the heavy oak door.

Mr. Bixby opened the door himself. He was a small man, barely five foot five with a head of thick, white hair. He sported a perpetual tan and wore expensive suits and ties. He had some eccentricities, but Rachel had grown fond of him over the years. He let her get on with her work and didn't interfere.

"Rachel, come in," he said, holding the door wide open for her.

Rachel walked in, taking in the glossy wood-grain paneling, the glass shelves in the bookcases, and the leather furniture. It not only looked expensive; it smelled and *felt* expensive as well.

She looked up and noticed there was another man seated in one of the two chairs in front of Mr. Bixby's antique desk. Upon her entrance, he immediately stood up.

Hesitating, she looked around. Mr. Bixby swept his arm in the direction of his desk. "Please, Rachel, take a seat."

She felt the eyes of the stranger on her, and she took a minute to assess him. Tall, mid-thirties, clean-cut, clean-shaven with thick, dark hair. His broad shoulders filled out his suit jacket. But it was his eyes—a deep blue, like an azure. They were startling. She paused. His eyes alone made him swoon-worthy. She wondered what his problem was. She couldn't wait to solve it.

Mr. Bixby stood between them. The other man towered over her boss. Even at her own height of five eight, she had to look up at the dark-haired man. Her curiosity went into overdrive: she couldn't wait to hear what this was all about.

"I'd like to introduce you to Rachel Parker, our Girl Wonder. First one here in the morning and last one to leave at night," Mr. Bixby said. "Rachel, I'd like you to meet Thomas Yates, Earl of Glenbourne."

Her eyes widened. She had never met a member of the realm before. Wait until she told her mother. Aware of his eyes on her, she extended her hand to him. "Nice to meet you," she said.

"The pleasure is mine," he said. He had a lilting foreign accent. Not British, but close. She watched a lot of BBC news. They delivered all the bad news the same way: as if they were going to serve you a cup of tea as the world went up in flames. It was oddly reassuring.

"Irish?" she asked, taking a guess.

He smiled and bowed his head slightly.

The gesture was a nice touch.

"Sit down, sit down, let's talk business," Mr. Bixby said. "The earl has brought us a problem."

"We're happy to help," Rachel said to him as they sat down.

"I'm hoping your reputation and your company are up to the task," the earl said. He glanced at his hands and then his gaze shifted back to her.

Rachel looked over at her boss, but he had been distracted by the paper tape streaming from the reproduction stock ticker. It sat under a glass dome atop a walnut pedestal. The repo ticked continuously. Mr. Bixby picked up the tape that had spooled in a pile on the floor and held it between his fingers for a moment, studying it with a frown.

"Mr. Bixby?" Rachel said, drawing him back to the moment.

"Yes, right," he laughed. "I have always found that sound quite relaxing." Dropping the paper tape, he made his way over to his chair and parked himself behind the desk. "When I go to bed at night, I have a machine that plays a continual *ka-ching* noise, and I drift off to sleep at the sound of money being made."

"I prefer the sound of wind and rain myself," said the stranger with the delicious accent.

Me too, thought Rachel.

"As I was saying, the earl has come to us with a problem," Mr. Bixby said.

Taking charge of the conversation, she turned in her seat to face the earl. "Lord Glenbourne, what is your problem, exactly?"

Slowly, he turned toward her and laid his magnificent blue eyes on her. "Miss Parker, I need a wife," he said. "And I need one right away."

Rachel blinked. The Earl of Glenbourne needed a wife and thought Bixby International could find him one? At first, she didn't understand why he would need help finding a wife. He ticked all the right boxes: tall, dark, and handsome. His posh accent was a bonus. But if he had a personality defect, that would explain a lot of things. Her mind went over a laundry lists of turnoffs: abusing animals, hating kids, not changing your underwear or socks daily.

She gave him a reassuring smile, ready for the task at hand. "Well, I've never played matchmaker before, but I assure you, I will find you a lovely wife."

The earl shook his head. "No, you don't understand. I don't have time to search for a proper wife."

She looked over at her boss, confused. Mr. Bixby sat with his hands folded on his desk and had a benign look on his face.

"I'm sorry—I'm confused," she said, looking from one to the other.

"Lord Glenbourne is bound by a family stipulation," Mr. Bixby started.

The earl spoke up. "I am the 12th Earl of Glenbourne. I own a large estate in Ireland that has been in the family for several centuries. The 6th Earl of Glenbourne, to encourage his unwilling son to get married to keep the line going, instituted a condition of the estate." He paused.

Rachel listened with interest.

Thomas Yates continued. "Every proceeding earl had to be married by the age of thirty-five or he would lose the money portion of the estate."

"Is that very important?" she asked. Money wasn't everything after all.

"Without it, I can't manage the costs or upkeep of the estate. By profession, I am a solicitor, but I don't make nearly enough to cover the costs."

"Oh." Ancestors were nice as long as they remained in the past. Her mind flooded with ideas. "Have you tried fighting this in court?" That was the most obvious one. After all, he was a solicitor.

"I am working on that, but no success as of yet."

"Who controls the money? Don't you?" she asked.

He shook his head. "The money for the estate is controlled by a trust. Has been since the 7th Earl of Glenbourne almost gambled the whole fortune away."

Despite his title and money, he had some dubious lineage.

"And you are unable to find a viable candidate in your own social circle?" she asked, finding this almost impossible to believe.

"No, I'm not interested in marriage as such. At least not yet," he explained. Up close, his eyes had depth and intelligence to them.

There were other problem solvers in the company. This was nothing more than Matchmaking 101. She began to feel her interest waning.

"When do you turn thirty-five?" she asked the earl.

"October first," he answered.

She couldn't help it; she burst out laughing. "You've certainly left it until the last minute. That's only a week away."

He shrugged, not seeming to care how he'd left it.

Mr. Bixby spoke up. "This is where we come in." Rachel couldn't wait to hear this part.

"After much discussion, we were hoping you could help him out," he said.

"Of course I'll help him out. That's my job," she said.

"That's great, Rachel! I told the earl that you were a team player and our best problem solver," Mr. Bixby said. "Now, you've got forty-eight hours to find the earl a suitable bride."

Rachel blinked. "That's not a lot of time."

The earl interrupted. "May I explain a few things that might help with your search?"

"Please do." She nodded and caught him glancing as she crossed her legs.

"I only need a wife for ninety days. After that, the condition on the trust expires. Of course, I will need her to live at my manor for those three months, but I guarantee that every whim of hers would be . . . um . . . satisfied."

Rachel raised an eyebrow. "And after the ninety days?"

"My 'wife' will fly back to the US and file for divorce. I will pay all expenses," he said.

"Why not divorce in Ireland?" she asked.

"Because divorce is only recently legal in my country, and a couple needs to be separated for four years before they can file for divorce," he explained. He paused, then said, "I wouldn't ask anyone to put her life on hold for that length of time."

"How thoughtful," she muttered. She glanced over at her boss, who sat at his desk with his hands folded on top of it.

"The earl has also agreed to sweeten the pot," her boss said.

Rachel looked back to the earl. Although he wasn't dangerously handsome in the windswept-moor kind of way one might expect from an earl, his bearing was regal.

"There will be a million-dollar bonus to anyone who would agree to marry me for the ninety days," he explained. "That should help you in your search."

"What are the terms?" she asked. If she was going to do this job properly, she needed all the facts and information at her disposal.

"Fifty percent down as soon as we are married and the remaining fifty percent at the end of the ninety days," he replied.

She nodded. "That's good. That will be a good enticement."

Thomas Yates continued. "We'd need to get married in New York as the registrar in Ireland requires three months' notice."

Rachel stood up from her chair. "I better get to work on finding you a bride." The earl stood up as well and extended his hand. His grip was firm and warm, and his hand dwarfed hers. It felt protective. Goosebumps rose on her arms.

Mr. Bixby stood up from his desk and said, "Let's meet back here in forty-eight hours." He looked directly at the earl. "I can assure you that Rachel Parker will have an acceptable solution to your problem in two days' time." He looked at Rachel, smiled benevolently and then turned to the earl. "In fact, I guarantee it."

Rachel wished she shared her boss's confidence.

It was dark by the time Rachel powered down her desktop computer. Sighing, she grabbed her purse and headed out of the office, noticing once again that she was the last one to leave. At the other end of the hall, she saw Lois, the nightly cleaning woman. When she saw Rachel, she made a face, pointed to her watch, and shook her head. Even the cleaning woman thought she worked too hard. But Rachel loved her job, so it wasn't like working at all. Actually, she preferred working at night when the office was quiet and there was no one else around. Less interruptions meant more work. As she stepped into the elevator and the doors slid closed on the semi-darkened office, she could hear the buzz of Lois's vacuum cleaner at the other end of the floor.

After her meeting with her boss and the Earl of Glenbourne, she'd spent the rest of the day researching and laying out parameters for her search. It was proving almost impossible. But she wasn't willing to admit to defeat just yet. After perusing some of the more ethical and upscale dating sites, she'd found some potential prospects, but there were two problems: time, and issues regarding privacy. You could get around the privacy issue by having them sign a non-disclosure agreement and rendering the million-dollar bonus null and void if there was a breach. But there simply wasn't enough time to vet someone properly.

She pushed it out of her mind. Best to tackle it again tomorrow when she had a clear head.

But first, she had a stop to make on her way home.

Gatefield Rehabilitation Center was a facility specifically for the rehab of a variety of medical problems from knee replacements to traumatic brain injuries. Glancing at the clock on her dashboard, Rachel saw that she'd only have a bit of time before visiting hours ended. She locked her car and walked at a rapid clip toward the building. Drawing in a deep breath, she pushed through the front doors. She nodded at the receptionist at the desk, signed in, and headed toward the back of the facility.

More than anything, Rachel hated hospitals and nursing homes. Dreaded them. The sanitized smell that could never quite do its job properly. To her, they all smelled like sickness and death. All the noises: the constant beeping, the chatter at the nurses' stations, the endless overhead pages—it was all too much stimulation.

Clutching the strap of her purse, she arrived at the last door of "B" corridor. Taking a deep breath and plastering a smile on her face, she knocked gently on the door before poking her head around it.

There in the chair sat her best friend since kindergarten, Amy Wagner Brzynski. Her long blonde hair was in a messy ponytail, and there were dark circles under her eyes. In the hospital bed beside her was Amy's husband of ten years, Brian. The previous year, he had been involved in a freak accident while on a ladder cutting down tree branches. One had gone astray, knocking him down, and he'd landed on his head, resulting in a severe brain injury. Many months had been spent in the hospital with Amy at his side. He'd been in rehab for just as long. He had to learn how to speak again and walk again. He'd never get back to where he was, but he was making slow progress. They had two young sons at home, and the whole thing was absolutely heartbreaking.

Amy's face broke into a generous smile. "Rachel!"

"Don't get up," Rachel said, going over and hugging her friend. She turned toward the bed and saw that Brian was sound asleep. Therapy all day wore him out. Rachel laid her hand gently on Brian's, not wanting to wake him. She looked at her friend. "How was his day?"

"Exhausting," Amy sighed and in that one sigh, Rachel heard her friend's anxiety, sorrows, frustrations, and worries of the past year.

Rachel sat in the chair next to her friend and crossed her legs.

"The specialist came in today and said that at some point we need to think about Brian's future," Amy said, bursting into tears.

Rachel reached out for her friend's hand and listened attentively.

"I have two choices: Brian can come home, or he'll have to go to a nursing home for long-term care." Amy cried harder.

"Okay," Rachel replied, trying to process what it meant for her best friend, her husband, and their two children.

"You know my family, Rachel; we always take care of everyone at home," Amy said.

Rachel nodded, remembering the Wagner household growing up. It was noisier and busier than her own. There was always a grandparent or two or a shirttail relative living with them. It had been normal to see visiting nurses at their house. It's what the Wagners did: take care of everyone. It came as no surprise to Rachel that Amy would want to take her husband home.

"I've been racking my brain all day trying to figure out how to take him home. I'd need all sorts of equipment as well as help." Amy voiced what Rachel was already thinking. "You know my house isn't exactly suited for Brian in this condition."

Rachel nodded. Amy and Brian were still living in their first home, and it was tiny. Three bedrooms. She didn't know where Amy would set Brian up. He'd need his own room. Not to mention the fact that getting him around the house in a specialized wheelchair would require some space to maneuver.

Rachel bit her lip. "I'll think about it as well."

"He's my husband. I love him. I just want to take him home." Amy laid her head on Rachel's shoulder and sobbed.

Rachel held her. Her mind spun, trying to figure out the best way to help her friend.

CHAPTER TWO

THE FOLLOWING MORNING, RACHEL spun her chair around and stared out her office window. Yawning, she focused her gaze on the building across the way. It didn't have any significance; she just needed something to stare at. So she could think. She had lain awake most of the night, wrestling with Amy's problem and the Earl of Glenbourne's need for a wife.

Shutting her eyes, she got comfortable in her chair by relaxing her shoulders and folding her hands in her lap. In her one hand, she clicked a pen. Her office door was always kept slightly ajar. The drone of office chatter, phones ringing, and the intermittent bursts of the copier just outside her office served as white noise.

Around and around the problems went like a merry-go-round. She had just spent half a morning going through a list of candidates she'd sourced from local dating sites. But after running them through her pre-application checklist, she had come up empty. Desperate, she'd looked at all the female employees at Bixby International. The single ones. But asking an employee to marry a complete stranger might break some laws. Then she went through her alumni directory from college. Most of the women had high-powered positions, and those that didn't were happily married, at home with children at their feet.

With her legs crossed, she rolled her pen between her fingers. She'd do it herself if she weren't afraid of flying. Or if she didn't suffer from terrible homesickness. The bonus alone would make it worthwhile. That would definitely sort out Amy's problems.

Her pen fell to the floor.

Why can't I marry him? It's only for three months!

All sorts of objections and protests blew through her mind. Ignoring them, she turned her chair back around to face her desk. Tapping her pen on her desk, a spark of excitement popped. This happened every time she came up with a solution to a problem. She pulled the contract from a pile and began to study it. It was the first thing she'd done after she'd left her boss's office: draw up a contract for whomever would fit this bill. She'd figured she could work back from there.

The confidentiality clause would be no problem. Rachel was lots of things, but she wasn't a blabbermouth. But trying to explain herself to her family would be tricky. They all knew about her fear of flying. But she'd get around it. Then there was the part about playing the earl's wife in public. It would be difficult to fake intimacy in public. By the end of her last relationship, she had had trouble faking the fact she even liked her boyfriend. Her sparse dating history came to mind. She had been unlucky in love. Just could never find the right one. She had resigned herself to the fact that she would be single, and she was perfectly okay with that. She loved her job, she had a nice home, and she was very close to her family. She was content. But this opportunity gave her the chance to experience being married for a little while. In her old age, when her nieces and nephew came to visit her in the nursing home, she'd be able to smile and tell them how she had been married to an earl for three months. That might prove to be a worthy experience.

But she had to think things through. Thomas Yates was desperate for a wife. And that gave her some leverage. If she did it, there'd have to be some conditions.

Thomas glanced at his watch. Rachel Parker was five minutes late. He was more than curious to see who she'd come up with on such short notice.

"Don't worry, Lord Glenbourne. Our Rachel will have a brilliant solution," Mr. Bixby reassured him.

He hoped so. Thomas continued to pace after declining an offer to sit down. The clock was ticking. It was less than a week until he turned thirty-five.

There was a firm knock on the door, followed by the entrance of Rachel Parker. She was a tall, slim woman with long, dark hair, dark eyebrows, and dark eyes. She wore a solid-colored pencil skirt with a print blouse. Though she was tall and wore heels, she still didn't meet the earl's height.

Carrying a pile of manila folders in her left hand, she extended her right hand to him, smiling. "Lord Glenbourne, it's good to see you again." When she smiled, her whole face lit up. Up close, her skin was creamy, and there was a constellation of freckles across her nose.

"Likewise," he replied. She had a good grip.

She laid her manila folders on her boss's desk. Turning to Thomas, she said, "I think I may have come up with a plausible candidate."

"I'm glad to hear it," he said, trying to mask the relief in his voice.

"Rachel has never let anyone down," Mr. Bixby piped in from behind his desk.

"Won't you sit, please," she said, indicating one of the chairs with a gesture of her hand.

Once they were seated, Thomas looked at her expectantly.

She drew in a deep breath. "Let me begin by saying that I've identified two problems with your request. The first is time. There isn't enough time to properly identify and find an appropriate spouse and vet them at the same time."

"Would they need to be vetted? It's only three months," he pointed out. There really was no need to complicate matters.

"What if someone had a lot of debt? Or a disreputable background?" she said. "Although I don't think you'd be responsible for it, it might give you a black eye in the press."

He sighed. "That's the last thing I want. Unfortunately, I'm an object of attention in the press back home." He brushed his fingers along his mouth, cupping his jaw. "And the second thing?"

"The second thing is confidentiality. Although we would require the candidate to sign a non-disclosure agreement and make the bonus conditional on it, there's no guarantee that she wouldn't sell her story after the bonus was fully paid out. You're in Ireland; she's over here. Can we be sure that your privacy won't be violated? That she won't someday tell the world it was all a sham?"

Thomas winced at the use of the word "sham." He considered himself to be honest and trustworthy. "Have you not found a bride for me yet?" He saw Bixby glance at her.

"Actually, I have found someone that I think might work well," she said with a smile.

Her boss smiled at her.

"Me," she said.

"You?" Thomas said.

"Yes, I'm suggesting myself for the three-month position," she said.

Mr. Bixby slapped the top of his desk. "Brilliant! Absolutely brilliant, Rachel."

Thomas was doubtful and refrained from comment. He had expected someone a bit more glamorous. Not that Rachel Parker wasn't attractive. She was. In a wholesome, girl-next-door kind of way. But he lived on an estate, and there were no girls next door. There was no next door. Based on her professional appearance, he didn't know if she could pull off the role of Lady Glenbourne.

Her smile disappeared. "Do you find fault with the idea?"

"She's perfect!" Mr. Bixby said at the same time. "I'm sorry I didn't think of this myself!"

The earl quickly shook his head. How did he explain this without offending her? "No, I was looking for someone . . . ah . . . a bit closer to my own social circle."

She tilted her head and her hair fell like a drape down the front of her shoulder. "Then I would suggest that you look for a wife in that social circle." She turned away from him, her back stiffened.

"Miss Parker, I certainly did not mean to offend you," he said, stepping closer to her. Her perfume was something light and flowery.

"Too late," she replied.

He scratched the back of his head and lifted his eyebrows. It was only for three months. And her arguments had been valid. Finally, he said, "Tell me the details."

Without looking at him, she opened up several of the manila folders, and like an illusory artist, she picked up piece after piece of paper, explaining everything in detail. She finished with, "We can go apply for the marriage license today and be married tomorrow in a civil ceremony."

And just like that, all his problems would be solved.

"However, I do have a few personal conditions of my own," she said. There was a slight tremor in her voice, and he looked up at her sharply.

"And they are?"

She handed him a neatly printed list. He scanned the list, raising an eyebrow.

The Earl of Glenbourne must pay his wife one compliment per week.
One night a week, he has to cook a meal for her.
In public, he has to hold her hand. But absolutely no kissing.

He rolled his eyes. "I don't cook, and I don't do public displays of affection."

She responded sweetly, "If you want a wife, then I guess you'll have to learn."

Mr. Bixby stood up, beaming, with his hands in his pockets. He shook his head. "Rachel, you've really outdone yourself this time. What a team player."

"Thank you, Mr. Bixby." She smiled at her boss.

"You should be running this place, not me," her boss crowed. He turned toward the earl. "I told you she was our star player."

Thomas looked at Rachel and then over at her boss, wondering if he had just been duped.

"I will draw up the documents, of course, for signing this afternoon. Afterward, we'll head over and apply for the marriage license."

He nodded, not quite believing that he was going through with this. But it was only temporary; in three months, things would go back to the way they'd always been. And Rachel Parker would return to the US.

The Earl of Glenbourne left the offices of Bixby International somewhat satisfied. With less than a week to go, he was on his way to saving his estate. He wouldn't celebrate until they were actually married.

They signed all the necessary documents, including the financial arrangement, which stated that half a million dollars would be transferred to Rachel's bank account the day after their marriage and the remainder at the end of the three months. He couldn't help but wonder if her motive was purely financial. Although it was a major enticement, he would have wondered that about anyone who had signed up for the task.

The two of them cabbed it over to the city clerk's office to apply for a marriage license. It all seemed straightforward. They had agreed that Rachel and Mr. Bixby would pick Thomas up at his hotel in the morning, and the three of them would drive back over to the city clerk's office, where Mr. Bixby would serve as their witness.

Rachel Parker, though reasonably attractive with all that dark hair and those big, expressive dark eyes, was something of a plain Jane. There was minimal makeup, and her clothes would set no fashion house on fire. She would not have been someone Thomas would have chosen. But on further thought, he figured she might be okay. She might not be glamorous, but her looks were wholesome and her reputation beyond reproach, according to her boss. Thomas hoped so. The last thing he needed was a scandal that might affect his family name.

He took a cab back to his hotel, taking in the sights and the sounds of the city. He loved visiting New York, and he certainly enjoyed the commotion, but he was always happy to go home to his own bed.

There was another reason that this marriage would provide relief, other than that stipulation of the trust. The press. He had grown tired of being labeled "Ireland's most eligible bachelor." The situation had become desperate. Any photo of him with a member of the opposite sex of marriageable age increased speculation.

As the cab pulled up in front of his hotel, he hoped that, in keeping with the glowing recommendation from the CEO of Bixby International, Rachel Parker was up to the task of playing the role of the Countess of Glenbourne for three months.

"I know, Mom, but it's only for three months," Rachel explained as she piled clothes next to her suitcase, which lay open on her living-room sofa.

Her mother's lips pressed into a thin line. "Well, I think it's wrong of Mr. Bixby to expect you to swan off to another country at the last minute. I mean, you have your own family obligations."

Rachel looked at her mother. "Babysitting my nieces and nephew on a regular basis does not constitute family obligations to him. If I had my own husband and children, then maybe."

At present, her two nieces, Molly and Kara, aged five and four, jumped vigorously on the sofa.

"Girls, please don't jump," Rachel's mother said. "You'll get hurt."

Neither girl listened, and they continued to jump, their long, dark hair flying all over the place.

Rachel had not told her parents, or anyone, that the day before, she had married the Earl of Glenbourne in a ten-minute ceremony at the county clerk's office. The bride wore business casual. She and the earl had exchanged hellos and then vows. The groom, without even looking at her, had slipped a thin gold band on her finger. There was no stopping for a drink or even a bite to eat. Thomas Yates had a plane to catch to Ireland from JFK later that evening, and Rachel went back to work. September in New York was always beautiful, and her wedding day had proved to be no exception: it had been sunny, clear blue skies and seventy-five degrees. And yet, the whole affair had depressed her.

"Jason, will you look up the weather in Ireland for me?" Rachel asked her twelve-year-old nephew. The oldest of the brood, he was quiet like Rachel's brother and her father.

Looking up from his phone, he nodded, and his fingers did a mad scramble across the screen.

Her mother continued to grumble as she helped her pack.

Rachel would have liked to have her own family one day, but as she headed into her thirties, she wondered if it would happen for her. Her favorite places to hang out, namely the bookstore or the library, weren't exactly hotbeds of single hookups. But she'd made peace with her single status a long time ago. If she married, fine, and if she didn't, that was fine, too. She wasn't the kind of person to marry just anyone simply for the sake of getting married. And yet she had done just that. She sat on the edge of the sofa, holding a cardigan in her hands. There she was, preparing to travel three thousand miles to pretend to be the wife of a man she hardly knew. And what was wrong with this man that he couldn't find a bride of his own? A real one?

Amy and Brian came to mind, and the thought renewed Rachel's sense of purpose and determination. She'd already hired an architect who specialized in accessible homes. Amy was going to take Brian home and have every comfort and piece of equipment needed to care for him. There'd also be staff to assist, so Amy could go back to work. Rachel had it all planned out. Amy had cried in her arms when she'd told her what was going to be happening. Rachel had opened up a bank account that was strictly for Amy and Brian. When she had checked the account that morning, she was pleased to see the money had been transferred. On the way to work, she had gotten a bank draft for the architect. There was already a meeting scheduled between Amy and the architect. They'd have to source a lot where they could build their new house, but Amy and the architect could do all that. When her friend had questioned her about the source of the money, Rachel had simply told her that it was a bonus for a complicated job. Amy had raised her eyebrows but said nothing.

Rachel looked over at her father, eating a slice of pie and sipping at his coffee. He hadn't said much. But then her father didn't say too much anyway. Her mother was the one who did all the talking.

"Three months is a long time to be gone," her mother said.

Rachel sighed. "I'll be back home before you know it." She wouldn't tell her mother yet that she would have to spend Christmas in Ireland. She hadn't wanted to think about it herself. One blow at a time.

Her mother shook her head in disbelief. "Doesn't Mr. Bixby know you have a life?"

The blame was not with her boss. Yes, Rachel had a life, not exactly as she had wanted it, but it was a flexible one. She focused on fitting everything into the suitcase. She'd seen a YouTube video on how to pack a suitcase properly, and she'd been able to pack more things than she'd expected.

Jason sidled up next to her. Without taking his eyes off his phone, he said, "Aunt Rachel, it's mostly a rainy, moderate climate. The highs in the summer are in the seventies and the lows in the winters are in the thirties."

She tousled his hair and he looked up at her with a frown. "Oops, sorry." She smiled. Almost a teenager, he was way beyond those types of childish things.

Her mother was behind her, removing clothes from a laundry basket to sort and fold. "If I were you, I'd go in there and tell your boss in no uncertain terms that this trip would be a hardship for you."

Rachel laughed. Her mother had always been her biggest ally, but sometimes she could be a bit over the top. "It's not really a hardship, Mom. I mean, there are a lot of people who would kill for an opportunity like this—to travel to Ireland," she said, wishing she was one of them.

Her mother raised her eyebrows while folding a pair of Rachel's pajamas. "Still, I think it's rude of him to expect you to disrupt your life for three months at the last minute."

As a child, Rachel had suffered terrible homesickness, and at sleepovers with friends or classmates, her parents were always called in the middle of the night to come and pick her up. But even this did not constitute a hardship.

As she looked around at her townhouse, a lump formed in her throat. This had been her home for the past five years. She had been so proud when she had purchased it. It had been empowering for her to do something that big on her own, with no help, before the age of thirty. Her stomach twisted into knots when she realized she wouldn't see it again until after Christmas.

Kara, the younger girl, fell off the sofa and hit her back against the leg of a chair. Immediately, she stood up and announced, "I'm not hurt." But her quivering chin said otherwise.

Rachel bent down. "Let me take a look, pet." There was no mark on her niece's back, but Rachel gave it a reassuring rub. "It'll be as good as new. Now, how about a snack?"

Kara nodded, still unconvinced about her back.

Molly yelled, "I want one, too!"

The girls climbed up on chairs next to Rachel's father, who tweaked their noses. Rachel poured juice and set out a plate of cookies, and the girls helped themselves.

Her mother continued to complain. Rachel had to tune her out. There was going to be no placating her over this. She liked her family around her, nearby. They were a close-knit clan and spent a lot of time together. And now, one of her ducks was traveling to the other side of the big pond.

Rachel looked over again at her father, who had remained silent the entire time. He had finished his pie and coffee and was rinsing his dishes in the sink.

"Dad?" Rachel prompted.

He turned around, leaning against the sink. He was pushing seventy, and his once-dark hair had seemingly gone gray overnight. Her father was a quiet, kind man. She could barely remember him ever raising his voice.

Her mother stopped folding laundry and looked toward her husband as well.

"Well?" her mother asked. "Don't you agree that this is a big inconvenience for Rachel to have to swan off to Ireland for three months?"

Rachel's father sighed and looked directly at his daughter. "Do you want me to tell you what you want to hear, or will I give you my own opinion?"

Rachel swallowed hard. When her father said this, it usually meant he was going to swim against the tide that was her mother and dole out a dose of some honest advice.

"Dad, I value your opinion."

He folded his arms across his chest and looked briefly at his wife, then back to Rachel.

"Then I think that this is a once-in-a-lifetime opportunity, and you would be stupid not to take it."

Chapter Three

Thomas Yates, the 12th Earl of Glenbourne, stood with his back to his desk, staring out of the floor-to-ceiling bay window overlooking the grounds of the thirty-thousand-acre estate that had been in his family for over four hundred years.

Rachel Parker, his "wife," was due to arrive late morning. Glancing at his watch, he figured her plane had landed by now in Dublin. It was a ninety-minute drive from the airport. He had been keen to pick her up, but she had refused, stating there was no need for that because she wanted to get a rental car for herself. He had offered her one of his cars from the stable, but she had refused that, as well. She'd explained she preferred to make arrangements for a rental car for herself.

Her impending arrival left him uneasy. It was one thing to consent to an arranged marriage, but it was something else to have to live with that person. And despite the fact that the manor was big enough that they might not have to see each other at all, it was bound to be awkward.

On the return flight, he'd given this some consideration. To keep both the gossip mill and the press at bay, they'd have to put on some appearance of a married couple. After all, he did have to live in this village. Fortunately, his job as a corporate lawyer for a multi-national company in Dublin would keep him busy and out of the way for at least some of the time. He wouldn't say he loved his job, but he loved the law. It allowed him to work remotely from the manor a few days a week. He had a secretary, a widowed woman from the village, Mrs. Maher, who handled all the administrative tasks. He had given her the day off and cleared his own calendar.

Now that he was married, a sense of relief flooded him despite the marriage bringing its own set of issues. This should get the press off his back. He was tired of not being able to talk to any female between the ages of eighteen and forty without a follow-up in the national newspapers with captions like, "Is She the One?" It had reached the breaking point over the summer when a photo of him with his colleague's daughter at a company picnic had been splashed all over the papers, and he'd been left to explain to her irate father that nothing was going on between him and the man's eighteen-year-old daughter.

When the plan of a marriage of convenience was first an idea, he'd decided not to bring an Irish girl into it. The country was too small: only four million people and everyone knew everyone. No, an American would be perfect. From a much bigger country, she'd be a virtual unknown here.

Percy, his butler, walked in. The butler had served his father for years, and though he was nearing seventy, the man was spry. Thomas had seen him more than once ascending the grand staircase at a rapid clip. He had a shock of silver hair that formed a widow's peak on his forehead.

"Sir, Mr. Bolton-Wright is here."

"Show him in," Thomas said.

The tall, lanky figure of his best friend and the master-mind behind this whole affair soon emerged from the hall. His best friend from Trinity, Sammy Bolton-Wright, had suggested Thomas opt for what had been done in the past: an arranged marriage. Initially, Thomas had thought the idea stupid, but then he had been so desperate for a solution that Sammy's plan had soon become the only option. Besides, he'd reminded himself, his own great-grandfather had married an American heiress when the funds had gone dangerously low, injecting some much-needed wealth into the estate.

Sometimes Thomas envied his mate. He wasn't landed or titled but seemed very happy with his lot in life. Granted, his parents were self-made millionaires from an online stationery shop they'd created over two decades prior, but Sammy didn't have the burden of obligation to one's heritage.

"Tommy!" Sammy called out. For as long as Thomas could remember, Sammy had always been loud and boisterous. He was the opposite of Thomas, who'd at times been accused of being abrupt, aloof, and snooty. Sammy had said on more than one occasion that his sole purpose in life was to "humanize" Thomas. And Thomas's response had always been the same: a smile and a laugh.

"Is tea all right?" Thomas said.

"It's fine," Sammy said.

Mrs. Brennan, the housekeeper, had set up a tea service on the table in front of the windows. Thomas looked out of the leaded-glass windows at the vast expanse of lawns, trees, and the last of the summer flowers. It was a sight he never tired of. The burden of his family history and its future lay squarely on his shoulders and no one else's. He remembered his parents' happy marriage and had just assumed he would have the same thing, but now, in his mid-thirties, that prospect seemed as elusive as ever.

He poured steaming-hot tea into two china cups and passed one to his friend.

Sammy took the teacup and raised it in the air. "To the new Countess of Glenbourne Manor."

Thomas paused and said, "Very funny, Sammy."

"When does the American arrive?" Sammy asked.

"I'm expecting her any time now."

"What's her name?"

"Her name is Rachel Parker," Thomas explained, taking a large gulp of his drink.

"Is she pretty?" Sammy questioned.

Thomas shrugged. "I guess so."

"Well, that's a relief."

"You are so shallow." Thomas laughed.

His friend took a generous sip of his tea. "Like most men, I'm a visual creature. For the ruse to work, she'd have to be a stunner."

Thomas turned to him. "Would she?"

"Yes, it does matter, or the press won't buy it."

They were both quiet for a moment, and Sammy sank onto one of the two settees in front of the tall fireplace, stretching his long legs out before him. A small fire burned in the grate. Autumn had arrived, and the temperatures had started to drop. The problem was never the cold; it was always the damp.

Thomas occupied the settee across from him, anxious to stop thinking about the arrival of the American woman.

"Will there be a church service?" Sammy asked.

The earl shook his head. "No, that won't be necessary. No sense in dragging the church into our arranged marriage."

"That's a pity," Sammy said. "I love a good wedding."

Thomas looked at him. "I do believe you are having a laugh at my expense."

Sammy grinned. "Just a little one. Are you going to the fox hunt next weekend at the Stabler estate?"

Thomas shook his head. "No, I don't want to subject her to Teddy just yet."

"A wise decision," Sammy said. "But then I'll be stuck with Teddy Stabler, and you know how boorish he can be."

Thomas grinned. "I do. Good luck with that."

The Stablers were another dynasty from County Kildare. They were titled, like Thomas, but they were a newly formed peerage within the last two hundred years. An extremely wealthy family, there were no stipulations or conditions attached to their dynasty. Teddy Stabler had a stable of horses that he kept, one of which was a recent Cheltenham winner. The problem was, he liked to remind everyone in earshot of his good fortune. It grated on Thomas's nerves.

"Think of all the fun you'll miss," Sammy said with a grin.

Thomas picked up his cup and drained it. "That's what I am thinking of. Thanks, but no. I have better things to do."

"Sit around here all by yourself and brood over things?" Sammy asked pointedly.

Thomas could not be offended; there was nothing malicious about his friend. He raised his glass as if to say "touché," and said, "You know me too well."

"We should get together for a meal."

"That's what I was hoping."

"Maybe you could bring your bride," Sammy said.

"Maybe. But doubtful. I'm hoping our personal lives won't mix. She is, after all, an employee on contract."

Sammy raised his eyebrows. "And who says romance is dead?"

"It has nothing to do with romance and everything to do with marriage."

"With that cheery take on marriage, it's no wonder you stayed single for so long."

"Just never found the right one."

"Change your mindset and you just might," Sammy suggested.

Thomas deftly changed the subject. "How is Trish?" he asked, referring to his friend's long-term girlfriend.

Sammy made a face. "Still squawking about marriage. It's starting to get old."

"Maybe you need to change your mindset," Thomas suggested.

Sammy laughed. "Not any time soon. I'll marry her someday."

"Don't let her get away," the earl warned.

"She's not going anywhere."

"I hope not," Thomas said, forcing his thoughts away from the subject of marriage.

Rachel drove into the picturesque village of Glenbourne, located south of the Wicklow mountains. She perked up at the sight of the colorful, little cottages with thatched roofs. Flower boxes overflowed with vibrant end-of-summer blooms. In the autumnal sunshine, the colors appeared golden-hued. She tried to take everything in and not get into an accident at the same time. There was an old stone church halfway along the main street, and most of the cottages had been turned into boutiques. She was curious about village life, and she'd make sure she got a walkabout. There was a visitor center next to the remains of an ancient castle.

There was so much to look at. She had never been outside of the United States before. And it was so different from the US. She had to drink it all in. All the road signs were in Gaelic and English. Everything was so old, unlike back home where it was a big deal if something had been around for two hundred years. She had received both her undergraduate and master's degrees in history, and this place was turning into a dream come true. Along the way to Glenbourne Village, she'd pulled over several times to look at crumbling ruins, mountain views, or cows grazing in stone-hedged fields.

As she came to the end of the village, she saw a high stone wall encompassing property that went on for at least a mile. Towering oaks were visible over the top of the wall, and at the end of the road was a small, gated entrance. A simple sign depicting a dynastic crest in bold colors read, "Glenbourne Manor," and beneath that in bold lettering were the words "NO TRESPASSING." Underneath, a smaller sign read, "Thomas Yates, Esq."

Slowly, she drove through the high gates, swallowing hard. The gate itself would probably cost her a whole year's salary. There was a long asphalt road cutting through the rolling green lawns and lush landscape. There was no sign of the manor yet, but from some quick research, she knew there were thirty thousand acres that belonged to the estate. The manor itself had been rebuilt in the nineteenth century from the ruins of the seventeenth-century manor, which had been destroyed in a fire. The grounds themselves were first mentioned in public records as far back as the sixteenth century.

As she crested a small hill, Glenbourne Manor came into view.

Her mouth fell open and she had to pull over to the side of the road and park the car. For a long while, Rachel just stared at Glenbourne Manor. It was an imposing Tudor Revival-style period house. Though the word "house" was woefully inadequate. The manor itself was styled in calendar form: it had 365 windows, fifty-two chimneys, and four wings. The current lord had been an only child. If he died without a son, his title would die with him. She hadn't even stepped foot into the manor itself, and her head was already doing a mass of calculations as to what it would cost to run this place. No wonder the earl was so dependent on the trust.

On first survey, she could see that the place was well tended: the leaded-glass windows gleamed, the flowers in the beds were vibrant and profuse despite it being the end of September, and the lawns, deep, rich, green, and rolling. She sighed and put the car back into drive. Luckily, pretending to be the wife of an earl was not a twenty-four seven job, and she couldn't wait to explore the place and learn of its history. She hoped beyond hope there was a library inside.

Directly in front of the manor was a circular, paved driveway. In the middle of that was a huge stone fountain with a stream of water gushing from it. She pulled her luggage from the trunk, set it down beside her, and stood there, getting an up-close look at the manor. A bit of apprehension assailed her. She hoped she was up to this task. Usually, when taking on a project at work, Rachel did exhaustive research not only to arrive at the best possible solution, but to learn as much background on the subject as possible. This was the first time in her ten years working at Bixby International that the solution came first and the research second.

She took it all in and immediately fell in love with the place. Reinvigorated by all that lay ahead of her to investigate, all thoughts and feelings of jet lag abandoned her and, pulling her luggage behind her, she ran up the steps of Glenbourne Manor, ready to play the part of Lady Glenbourne.

The Earl of Glenbourne watched from his window in the study as the rental car slowly pulled up to the front of the manor. Rachel stepped out of her car and looked around before pulling her luggage behind her toward the entrance. He turned away from the window.

"Is she here?" Sammy asked.

"She is."

"Do you want me to leave? It feels awfully intrusive. Maybe you should meet her alone."

The earl shook his head. "No. A neutral buffer will be needed."

Sammy made a mock, sweeping bow. "As you wish, my lord."

Thomas laughed.

Percy entered the room and announced, "Miss Parker, my lord."

The earl watched keenly as Rachel entered the room, ready to see her in the Glenbourne Manor surroundings and see if he would be able to pass her off as his new bride. Her long, dark hair fell below her shoulder. Her large brown eyes, at that moment, appeared wary. There was scant makeup on her face. Again, she wasn't the type of girl he usually dated. But she would do for this short-term project.

Confidently, despite the frightened look in her eyes, she stepped forward, extending her hand. "Lord Glenbourne, good to see you again."

There was a shock of static electricity when their hands met. She laughed. "Must remember not to drag my feet across the carpet. I certainly wouldn't want to electrocute the Earl of Glenbourne!"

Sammy laughed behind them.

"No, that would not do," the earl agreed. "Please, call me Thomas, and this is my friend, Sammy Bolton-Wright."

He watched as she shook Sammy's hand and scrutinized her surroundings. It was all done up in dark woods: cherry, walnut, and mahogany. There were paneled walls and bookcases crammed with textbooks and law books. Plush, red-velvet settees were grouped around the hearth along with two leather club chairs. At the back of the room was the large executive desk where he worked. The study was Thomas's favorite room in the house; it was—what was the term the Americans used?—his "man cave." As a boy, he had crawled around his grandfather's feet as he had sat at his desk conducting estate business. This room was to him, simply put, "home."

"You must be very tired," he said. "Would you prefer to retire to your room for a bit to rest up? I know the jet lag traveling from west to east can be difficult."

"Thank you," she said. "I'll get my luggage."

He shook his head. "The luggage will already have been brought up to your room. I also had them take up some tea and something light to eat."

She smiled. Her smile was lovely and warm. "That's very kind. If it's all right with you, I will head upstairs and see you later."

"Of course," he said. Thomas walked over to the wall and pulled the long bell cord. "The housekeeper will show you to your room."

"Again, thank you."

The earl thought Sammy was unusually quiet, and he glanced at his friend and discovered he appeared dumbstruck. He rolled his eyes in response. Sammy appeared to be crushing on the American. Thomas scowled at him, but Sammy did not appear to notice.

Mrs. Brennan soon appeared and led Rachel out of the room.

As the door closed softly behind them, Sammy broke into a grin. "So that's the new countess."

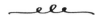

Rachel was overwhelmed. Blindly, she followed the housekeeper to the grand staircase, her neck craning as she tried to look at everything: high-paneled walls, paintings, tapestries, and sculptures. She chastised herself and told herself to calm down; there would be plenty of time to thoroughly investigate the place later. After all, she had three months to do it.

The presence of the earl's friend had caught her off guard. She had hoped her meeting with Thomas Yates would be a private one. But apparently, he'd felt the need for backup. He'd been dressed casually, the pullover sweater and jeans he wore showcasing a finely sculpted body. But he had appeared detached. She felt as if she had been caught on the back foot. Sammy, on the other hand, had a friendlier face with his red hair and hazel eyes, and she wished he were the earl instead. How on earth would this work out if the earl was difficult? Or worse, lacked personality and was dull? It might explain why he wasn't married. It would also make for a long three months.

She groaned out loud. The housekeeper turned sharply toward her. "Are you all right, Miss?"

"I'm fine," Rachel said. She placed one foot on the staircase and paused. "Just need to clarify something with Lord Glenbourne." And as the housekeeper protested and called out after her about needing to be announced before she walked into a room, Rachel dashed back to the earl's study.

Quietly, she opened the door to the library and saw that the two men were right where she'd left them. The earl had his back to her and was speaking to his friend, who noticed her return, his eyes widening.

"Well, she's average-looking in a girl-next-door kind of way. She isn't someone you'd give a second look—"

Rachel was stunned. She hadn't even been out of the room five minutes and her "husband" had insulted her. Shaking, she cleared her throat.

"Excuse me, I'm sorry to interrupt," she said, finding her voice. She stepped into the room.

Thomas spun around. A scarlet flush crept over his face.

"Rachel, I'm—" he started, but she cut him off.

"I wondered what time you wanted to meet up later to discuss the project?" she asked him. Anger coursed through her. Lifting her chin a bit, she didn't take her eyes off his face, forcing him to look directly at her.

"After lunch, if that's all right?" He had the decency to look embarrassed.

But Rachel wasn't going to let him off the hook that easy. Money certainly didn't buy manners.

"Could you be more specific? What time is lunch? Where is it served?" she shot. "Saying 'after lunch' is kind of vague, don't you think?"

The earl straightened up. "Lunch is served at one o'clock in the breakfast room."

"I'll be there," she said. She paused with her hand on the doorknob and turned back toward her so-called husband.

"What I would say about you, as far as looks go, is that without a doubt, you tick all the boxes." She made a point of giving him a once-over from head to toe. "However, after a short time in your presence, it's easy to see we are at the shallow end of the pool." Cheeks burning, she slipped out the door. It wasn't fully closed when she heard Sammy burst out laughing.

CHAPTER FOUR

R ACHEL WASN'T EVEN OUT the study door when the earl
caught up to her.

"Rachel," he said.

When she didn't stop, he reached out for her, laying his hand on her arm. His grip, though firm, was gentle.

"Rachel, *please*," he said.

She turned around to face him.

"I behaved abhorrently," he said. He seemed sincere.

She folded her arms across her chest. "And what type of woman would warrant a second look? Someone a bit more glamorous? Exciting? Prettier?" Suddenly, she was overwhelmed with exhaustion and anxiety and feelings of inadequacy.

His lack of response to her questions answered them. "Please accept my apology," he said. "There's no excuse for rudeness."

Wearily, she nodded and said, "Apology accepted," hoping to put it all behind her. She looked over to the grand staircase where the housekeeper waited for her, patiently. "Look, I'd like to go to my room."

"Of course," he said. He sighed. "Again, I am sorry."

Turning on her heel, she headed toward Mrs. Brennan.

When she reached the staircase, the housekeeper said in a clipped tone, "In this manor, we announce people walking into a room."

"Yes, I can see why that would be a good idea," Rachel muttered.

She followed the housekeeper in silence toward the second floor. It was a massive place, and she didn't know where to look first. There were tapestries and a gallery of paintings. All sorts of banners and the crest emblazoned across a flag hung from the vaulted ceiling above. As she wound her way up the staircase, she looked down at the main hall. There was a large, circular table with an enormous vase of fresh flowers on it.

At the top, on the landing, Mrs. Brennan proceeded down the first corridor. Rachel couldn't imagine calling a place like this home. There was nothing cozy about it. As impressive as it was, it was also a bit intimidating.

"Here we are," Mrs. Brennan said, stopping, pulling a key from the chain at her waist, and unlocking a door. She slipped another key from her pocket and handed it to Rachel.

"Here's a key to your room," Mrs. Brennan said. She stepped back, holding open the door with her arm.

Rachel stepped into an expansive room, the size of which was greater than her whole townhouse. The room was done up in pink and white with a faded floral carpet that Rachel suspected had at one time been quite luxurious. As promised, there was a tea service set on the table by the fireplace. Tea steamed in a silver pot, and there were little cubes of white and brown sugar in a silver bowl. There was a plate of sandwiches, and scones with jam and cream. Her stomach growled in response. The airplane food had not agreed with her.

"I'll leave you to it," Mrs. Brennan said, closing the door.

Rachel surveyed the rest of the room that would be hers for the next three months. It was very luxurious, but it wasn't hers. She looked at the queen-sized bed with the complicated curtains hanging around it and longed for her own bed back home. Exhausted, she flopped down on the bed and burst into tears.

"That went well," Sammy said when Thomas returned to the study.

"Are you laughing at my expense?" Thomas asked.

"I am, as a matter of fact," his friend admitted. "It's nice to see that you make mistakes, too."

The earl closed his eyes and pressed his fingers to his forehead in a futile attempt to stave off a looming headache. "I've certainly put my foot in it."

"Both of them, if you ask me," Sammy said. "'Shallow end of the pool.' That was priceless."

Thomas said nothing; he was still mortified at his own behavior.

Sammy shrugged. "She's no shrinking violet, that's for sure. She came back fighting."

"To you, I suppose that is refreshing," the earl said.

"For her spunk alone, I might have to pledge allegiance to team Rachel."

"I'm delighted you find this amusing," Thomas said.

"I'm delighted I'm privy to this scheme of yours," Sammy said, sinking down onto the sofa. "It's like Christmas come early."

From the window, the earl could see Max, his Irish wolfhound, running up the lawn. He couldn't help but wonder what he had gotten into now. Thomas walked over to the doors that led to the terrace, opened one of them, and called for the dog. Once the animal heard his master's voice, the dog bounded toward him, tongue lolling out of the side of his mouth. The earl laughed at the sight of his pet.

The dog bounded in and the earl scratched him behind his ears. "What have you been up to this morning, Max? No good, I'm sure."

The dog went over and licked Sammy's face. Thomas's friend made a grimace of disgust, pulled a handkerchief from his pocket, and wiped his face. "Why couldn't you get a smaller dog, like a Corgi or a Jack Russell Terrier?" Sammy asked. He eyed the dog warily. "Something more manageable. This fella's a beast."

Thomas frowned. "We've always had large dogs," he explained, wondering why an explanation was needed anyway. Dogs were a personal choice, and everyone had the type of breed they preferred.

He sat down on the settee next to Sammy, and the dog lay down at his feet with a groan. Absentmindedly, the earl scratched the dog's head.

"Are you regretting it already?" Sammy asked.

Thomas shook his head. "No." But the thought of the American dressing him down indicated that she wasn't as docile as she appeared. With an amused smile, he said, "At least, not yet."

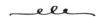

When Rachel awoke some hours later and looked around the vast room, she was confused. It took her a moment to get her bearings. Glancing at her watch, she saw that it was just past two in the afternoon. There was a tea service of floral china laid out on a table near the fireplace. Even though the tea had gone cold, she poured herself a cup, adding sugar and milk. Sipping it, she thought she'd ring her parents and let them know she had arrived safely. It would be just after ten in the morning on the east coast in the States.

Her mother picked up on the first ring. "How was your flight?"

Rachel answered, "Fine," choosing not to recount that white-knuckle adventure. It didn't bear thinking about that she'd have to get on another plane in a few months to go home, and she pushed the thought far out of her mind. But it didn't stop her from shuddering.

"Well, what's he like? The earl?" her mother asked. Despite her annoyance over her daughter being away for three months, she was a big fan of *Downton Abbey*, and she'd want to know every detail of how the other half lived.

"He's fine." Rachel glossed over their brief meeting upon her arrival earlier.

Her mother shot out a volley of questions as rapid as machine-gun fire. "How old is he? How tall is he? Do you have to curtsey?"

To which Rachel replied, "Mid-thirties. Six foot three or four. No, I do not have to curtsey."

"What's the manor like?"

"Big and grand. A butler and a housekeeper that I've seen so far."

Her mother made a noise of approval on the other end of the phone.

"How's Daddy?" Rachel asked.

"He's fine. He wants to talk to you," her mother said, and there were small noises on the other end of the line as the phone was passed to her father.

"Rachel, how's it going?" her father asked. Before she could answer, her father sputtered on, "Remember, we don't do titles here, so pay no mind to that nonsense. He puts his shoes on one at a time just like the rest of us. Don't forget you're an American."

Rachel let out a little laugh. No one liked to wave the flag more than her father. "No, I won't forget."

"That's all I wanted to say. I'll talk to you later," her father said, and then he was gone.

"Bye, Daddy," she said, her voice breaking. She held it together until she hung up the phone. She lay back down on the bed. Thoughts of home, her family, and her own bed flooded her mind. Everything was so strange and unfamiliar. A wave of homesickness swept over her.

Aware of the time, she stood up and wondered about a bathroom. She tried one door, but it was locked, and even after she tried the key, it remained locked. She'd have to ask about that. On the other side of the room was another door, and this led to an en suite bathroom.

After she showered and changed into a fresh set of clothes, she made her way downstairs.

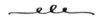

The earl sat at his desk in the study. Before him was plenty of paperwork that should have kept him quite busy. However, he had been unable to concentrate since Rachel had gone upstairs and Sammy had left. The incident earlier that morning had not been one of his finer moments. What had possessed him to make a passing comment on her looks? When he had realized she was standing right behind him and had heard his callous remark, the knowledge of his appalling behavior had made him contrite. But when he turned around and saw the wounded look on her face, he was utterly ashamed. He had spent the rest of the morning going over it in his mind. At first, he'd wanted to make amends, then he'd gone through a short-lived phase of "who cares?" Technically, she was an employee under contract. He finally settled on the idea that no matter what, she was still a guest in his home, and he would make sure he did everything he could to make her comfortable.

His ruminations were interrupted by a soft knocking on the study door.

"Come in," he called.

Rachel entered the room. There was some hesitation in her step, and she looked tired, he thought. He stood up and stepped out from behind his desk. *Your role as gracious host starts now*. Max also stood up and trotted over to Rachel, excited at the prospect of a new person to make a fuss over.

Rachel laughed as the dog approached. "Wow, you're a big dog."

The dog wagged his tail furiously and thought about jumping up on Rachel.

"Max," the earl said sternly.

The dog looked over his shoulder at his master and decided against jumping.

Irish wolfhounds were big dogs. Max himself stood three feet high at the shoulder and weighed in at a solid twelve stone.

Rachel continued to make a fuss over the dog, ignoring the earl. The dog, of course, was delighted.

"I trust you were able to rest," Thomas said. "Everything is to your liking?"

"Yes, of course. It's fine," she said. The dog sat down next to her, and Rachel gently massaged his ear.

"Will you join me for lunch?" Thomas asked.

She nodded.

"First, I thought I would introduce you to the staff," he said.

Rachel placed her hand at the base of her throat. Before she could protest, Thomas stepped back over to his desk, picked up the phone, and dialed a number. "Percy? Would you assemble the staff in the hall? I have an announcement to make."

"Just go along with me," he instructed. He held out his hand to her. She appeared to hesitate. He studied her. "I assure you, I mean you no harm. This is just for appearances' sake." He paused. "Besides, I think one of your conditions was that there was to be handholding in public."

"Of course." She placed her hand in his. He folded his hand over her smaller one. It was soft and delicate to the touch, which belied her true nature if earlier was anything to go by. Her hand was lost in his large grip. Together they strolled toward the main hall with Max trotting behind them. The staff were assembled in a line. Thomas sensed her nervousness and wanted to give her hand a reassuring squeeze, but something told him that that might be unwelcome.

Rachel's eyes widened at the sight of twenty-three staff members lined up before them.

The earl smiled at the manor staff. "I have some news. Good news, I assure all of you. I'd like to introduce you to Rachel Parker from New York." He paused and looked at her with what he hoped was a convincing smile. "We were married in New York City a few days ago."

The manor staff could not hide their surprise, and there were a few audible gasps down the line.

For effect, Thomas slid his arm around Rachel's waist. She stiffened under his touch, and he relaxed his hold a bit. He looked down at her and said with a smile, "I hope you will make my bride feel welcome in her new home." He looked at her in the way a groom would look at his new bride, or at least that was the effect he was going for. In response, she blushed.

Taking her by the hand, he led her over to the staff to introduce her to them. Turning toward Rachel, he asked, "How would you like the staff to address you?"

"'Rachel' is fine," she said.

Mrs. Brennan emitted a sound of disapproval.

The earl laughed. "We're not that informal at the manor."

Rachel's eyes did not leave Thomas's face. She performed her part perfectly. He thought they were pretty convincing.

"Will 'Lady Glenbourne' be all right?" he asked. All the previous earls' wives had been addressed as such. There was no reason why Rachel shouldn't be similarly called; after all, they were legally married, and she was entitled to the title.

She nodded. "That's fine."

He went down the line and introduced her to everyone: the cook, the under cook, the housemaids, the gardeners, and the sub-gardeners. It took a small army to run a place like Glenbourne, and his new wife looked overwhelmed.

With that out of the way, he figured lunch was in order. He led her down the hall.

"That went well, don't you think?" he asked her with a smile. "You were perfect! A little nervous. A little flushed. You were the perfect blushing bride."

As they walked down the gallery, Rachel looked up at all the paintings decorating the walls of the previous earls and their wives. Neither said a word.

Thomas felt compelled to make conversation. She was awfully quiet. It was possible she was still fuming over the morning's incident, or perhaps it was just her personality. He hoped it wasn't the latter. "Breakfast and lunch are always served in the breakfast room, and dinner is served at eight in the dining room," he said.

She nodded.

In the breakfast room, a buffet had been laid out on one of the sideboards. The earl held out his arm, indicating Rachel should go first. There were dishes of smoked salmon, cream cheese, brown bread, rocket lettuce dressed with tomatoes, corn, and shredded carrots, and there was a small tureen of soup. Lifting the lid, Rachel looked questioningly at the contents: an orange-colored soup.

He smiled and said, "Looks like carrot and parsnip. And it's excellent." She ladled some into her bowl and carried her plate and bowl to the table, where there were two place settings next to each other.

Initially, they ate their lunch in silence. To Thomas, her presence was magnified tenfold because of the awkward silence.

"Would it be better if I took my meals in my room?" she asked, her eyes bright.

He shook his head. "That would not do. How would it look if my wife spent all her time in her room? The staff would talk."

She looked disappointed. "Of course."

There was a tea set on the table. Thomas lifted the teapot and gestured toward her cup.

"Please."

He hesitated. "Would you prefer coffee instead? I know the Americans drink a lot of coffee."

Rachel shook her head. "The tea is fine. I only drink coffee in the mornings."

He poured tea into her cup. "Mrs. Brennan will go over your daily menu with you later, so we can have on hand any things you would prefer for breakfast and lunch. I usually let Mrs. Shortt decide on the dinner menu herself."

"Will we go over the project now?" she asked.

He hesitated and shook his head. "I would prefer to do it privately in the study."

"All right," she said with a sigh.

The earl looked up. "Is there something wrong with your food?"

She shook her head. "No, the food is delicious."

"It's just that you sighed."

Rachel's eyes widened. "No, no, everything is fine," she said. She appeared thoughtful for a moment. "It's difficult to eat a meal with someone you barely know."

He smiled. "Is it? I do it all the time."

"Never mind." She stared at her plate.

He lowered his voice but it was not unfriendly. "Please, explain."

Without looking at him, she said, "I'm not good at small talk with strangers."

"Would you prefer we didn't talk?"

"Oh no, that would be worse," she said. "I would not want to sit in stony silence with anyone. My mother's dinner table is pretty boisterous."

Silence descended. He had to agree with her. If they couldn't find something to talk about, it was going to be a painful three months. For both of them.

"Why don't we just concentrate on trying to get to know one another?" he suggested.

"Do you work full-time as a solicitor?" she asked. She cut up her smoked salmon and added a little cream cheese to it.

"I do. I work several days a week in Dublin, and I do work a few days a week from home."

And that was the end of that conversation.

The earl laid his knife and fork across his plate and pushed it away. He lifted the teapot and asked, "More tea?"

She nodded and laid a hand on his arm. She had long, slender fingers. "Am I supposed to be pouring the tea?"

Obviously, she had watched too much *Downton Abbey*.

The earl rewarded her with an amused smile. "Not necessary. I am quite capable of pouring the tea."

The lunch had been somewhat more than what Rachel was used to, so she refused dessert. The earl himself had forgone the offer of a rhubarb crumble and instead had a bowl of fresh fruit.

Instructions were given to Mrs. Brennan to bring more tea to Thomas's study. Rachel and Thomas walked side by side down the corridor toward his study. Rachel had already taken a shine to this room. Granted, she had only been in this room, the morning room, and her own bedroom, but she loved the warmth and coziness of the dark woods and heavy fabrics.

A fire blazed in the hearth, creating a warm, cozy atmosphere. Rachel thought it would be a great place to curl up with a good book on a rainy day.

At the back of the room was a map table with a big map of the world laid out. Rachel regarded it for a moment, thinking of all the places she'd never been. The earl rolled it up and set it out of the way.

Thomas pulled out a chair for Rachel, and she couldn't help but be impressed by his gentlemanly manners. Maybe he was redeemable.

"When will you make our marriage public?" Rachel started.

"In a couple of weeks. I thought I'd give you a chance to settle in," he explained. He leaned back casually in the chair. He was very handsome, and she tried not to be distracted by his looks. But it was almost impossible. His looks were classical: strong jaw, broad cheekbones, aquiline nose.

Rachel agreed with him. She studied him. How on earth did he think a fake wife and marriage would get the press off his back? It told her that he must have been at his wits' end to come up with this scheme. She didn't envy the fishbowl existence he led.

"I'll tell an abbreviated truth," he said. "I'll release a statement that we were married in New York City on September twenty-sixth and returned to Ireland to live."

The "returned to Ireland to live" had a ring of finality about it. She reminded herself that she would be going home in three months. *One day at a time.*

"Is that it?" she asked.

He looked at her. "Yes. It's succinct. What else do we need?" He began to spin his pen on the table, looking bored.

"It's brief, but it might not be enough."

"Well, it will have to be enough," he said.

"What about a honeymoon?" she asked.

He looked at her abruptly. His expression was hard to read. "Did you want to go on a honeymoon?"

She laughed. "No, of course not, but they'll expect us to. After all, we are supposed to be in love."

He looked thoughtful, his dark eyebrows knitting together in a frown. "We'll say we'll take a honeymoon at a later date."

She reread the press statement he had composed. "You don't want to add anything like 'after a whirlwind romance'?" she asked, sipping her tea.

He shook his head and laughed. "Definitely not."

"Why not?" she asked.

"Because that's what they want me to say," he said. Tapping his fingers on the desk, he regarded her for a moment. "You ask a lot of questions."

"I have to if I'm to solve people's problems," she answered.

"Do you like solving other people's problems?" he asked.

She nodded. "I like assisting people in finding all the options that are available to them."

"And you enjoy this?" he asked. He didn't seem like he was asking in disbelief but rather looking for clarification. "Why?"

"Yes, I do." As to the "why," she'd never given it much thought. "I suppose I like helping people."

For a moment, neither said anything.

"Can I ask about the stipulations of the trust?" Rachel asked.

"What in particular?" he asked, shifting in his seat.

"Is it public knowledge?" she asked.

He shook his head. "No, it isn't. I don't think even the staff know about it. Both my father and grandfather were married before thirty-five, so it didn't apply to them. I didn't know about it myself until my father was elderly. He told me before he died."

"And you didn't think to do anything about it?" she asked, trying to make her voice sound like she was not accusing him of anything.

He shrugged. "To be honest, I didn't give it much thought. I was busy with my life, and I just assumed I'd be married by now."

CHAPTER FIVE

L ATER THAT EVENING, RACHEL decided to skip dinner and changed into her pajamas and robe. A wave of homesickness rolled over her, and she longed for her own bed. The first day at Glenbourne Manor was behind her. Briefly, she toyed with the idea of making a paper chain, hanging it over her bed, and removing a link each night until she could go home. She couldn't fault the earl on any point; he had been nothing but polite since the debacle of the morning. He seemed to be going out of his way to make her feel comfortable. And she supposed that that alone was redemptive, which was promising.

Images of her home and her bedroom placed themselves front and center in her mind. She thought of her mother, her father, her brothers and their children, and the boisterous family dinners, where there was relaxed chaos with no worry about decorum or which spoon or fork to use.

The press release was going out from the manor within two weeks. And before those two weeks were up, she would have to inform her parents. She knew she really should call them and tell them she had married the earl, but she also knew if she heard their voices, she would start crying. There was plenty of time to call them and tell them the truth. Even though she dreaded it.

The bed had been turned down by one of the maids, and Rachel slipped her feet under the covers and leaned back against the ornate headboard. A carving dug into her back, and she placed a pillow behind her. She pulled a tissue from the box on the nightstand and blew her nose.

There was a knock at her door.

She got back out of the bed and opened it a crack. It was the housekeeper.

Mrs. Brennan ignored the state of her dress. "Dinner has been served in the dining room. Lord Glenbourne requests your presence."

You've got to be kidding me.

"I'll be right down."

Hurriedly, she pulled on the clothes that were lying in a pile on a nearby chair: a pair of jeans and a sweater. She wasn't really hungry, but she supposed she should eat something; it was a long time until breakfast, and it didn't seem the type of house where you could sneak down to the kitchen in the middle of the night to get a snack. Besides, she didn't even know where the kitchen was located. She made a mental note to get a few bags of candy in the village to keep in her room.

Thomas had just entered the hall when Rachel descended the staircase for dinner. He noticed that the light picked up shades of red running through her thick brown hair. The effect was quite beautiful against her porcelain skin and her brown eyes.

He smiled at her. He found himself wondering if she had a boyfriend back home. He couldn't see any boyfriend agreeing to this arrangement.

He wondered why he had made that terrible comment about her to Sammy. Maybe he had been feeling peevish at the thought of a guest in his home for three months, even if she was helping him out. Chiding himself, he realized that his passing comment was untrue. Because there he was, taking a second look.

He waited for her at the foot of the stairs. "Rachel," he said. He was aware of Mrs. Brennan lurking behind him and for appearances, he offered Rachel his arm, which she promptly took.

They walked arm in arm down the gallery, and he held open the door for her. Her eyes widened and her mouth opened slightly as she took in the dining room.

There were two marble-topped sideboards with ornate carvings and all sorts of silver serving dishes on top of them. A long mahogany table ran the length of the room, dominating it. The polished wood gleamed in the light from the massive Waterford chandelier that was suspended from the ceiling. Huge silver candelabras stood on the table, flowers and ribbons streaming from them.

With pride, Thomas watched as Rachel's eyes wandered up toward the mirrored ceiling with its heavy, ornate crossbeams that gave it a diamond pattern. At each intersection was a small crystal light in the shape of a star.

"Wow," she said.

The room was done up in various shades of green, with paintings that had been in the family for hundreds of years occupying walls covered in watered silk wallpaper. A giant Flemish tapestry hung over the main wall.

"This is gorgeous," she finally breathed.

Oddly, he was delighted she was pleased. "This was my mother's last project before she died. She had planned to give the whole manor an overhaul but died before she could finish it."

Rachel looked at him. "It would have been amazing to see what she could have done to the rest of the place." Then she added quickly, "Not that there's anything wrong with the rest of the manor, but this room is simply sublime."

He laughed. "I know what you mean."

There were two place settings at opposite ends of the long table.

"Would you mind if I moved my place setting closer to you?" she asked. "At this distance, we'd have to shout at one another."

"Of course not, sit wherever you like," he said, sorry he hadn't thought of that himself.

"Where do you sit?" she asked.

He nodded toward the seat at the head of the table.

She laughed. "Of course." She went to pick up the other place setting, but Thomas reached out and laid a hand on her arm.

"The staff can do that."

"There's no need; I'm right here," she said.

And before he could alert Percy, she picked up her utensils and napkin and handed them to Thomas, who had no choice but to accept them. She lifted her plate, water glass, and wine glass and carried them over to the seat next to Thomas. Copying his place setting, she set up her own. He found all this highly amusing. When she was finished, he pulled out her chair for her.

"Thank you, Thomas," she said, smiling up at him. She removed her napkin from the table and draped it over her lap.

The first course was a small bowl of potato-and-leek soup.

Rachel glanced at the earl, remarking, "I did not get the memo that we were to dress for dinner."

He shrugged and glanced at her. "It's done out of habit. I've dressed for dinner my whole life. But please, wear whatever makes you comfortable."

She giggled.

He smiled; her laugh was contagious. "What's so funny?"

"I just had an image of myself coming down in my pajamas and bathrobe." She laughed.

He started to laugh as well, but an image of her in a night-gown paraded across his mind, and this startled him. He looked at his fake wife and concluded it was a nice change to share his dinner with someone, instead of eating alone.

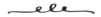

It had been a long day, and Rachel couldn't wait to climb into bed. Taking a wall calendar she'd brought from home, she flipped the pages until she reached October. She crossed off the day with a big, black X. *Day one of the hostage situation down; only eighty-nine more days to go*. That would take her past Christmas, but she didn't want to think about that. The thought of not spending the biggest holiday of the year with her family made her physically ill. Besides, all the emotion—or lack of it—of her first day at Glenbourne made her sleepy, and that made her prone to weepiness.

In the adjoining bathroom, she washed her face with cleanser, applied toner, slathered moisturizer on her face, and finished by brushing her teeth. Afterward, she dressed in a T-shirt with a faded logo and purple pajama bottoms and pulled her big, heavy pink robe around herself.

She pulled her hair up into a messy bun and collapsed on the bed. There was no television in the room, and she could really use a television right then. She wasn't in the mood for reading. There'd be no way she could concentrate, thinking of her parents and her family back home. There was an ache for them in the center of her chest.

It was while her thoughts were on her family back home that she thought she heard a knock on the locked door on the interior wall.

She sat up and listened. She must have been mistaken. Who on earth would be knocking on that door? She remained still and there it was again: a soft, gentle knock.

Standing up from the bed, she tiptoed over to the door and listened. When the knock came again, a bit more insistent this time, she asked, "Who's there?"

She thought she heard a chuckle on the other side. "It's me. Thomas."

She unlocked the door from her side, opened it and stepped back, placing her hand at the base of her throat. Thomas stepped into her room and closed the door behind him, but not before she had a glimpse of the room on the other side of the door. *His* room. It was done up in masculine colors of navy, gray, and dark woods. Before he'd closed the door, she saw that his bed had not been pulled down.

He wore a dressing robe over pajama bottoms and a T-shirt. She tried not to stare at his broad chest or the sculpted abs beneath his T-shirt. She didn't know where to look.

Then it dawned on her. Rachel took another step back, horrified. "You are not serious! You can't expect to consummate the marriage! I will not do it! I have to draw the line somewhere. Where was *this* in the contract?"

"Rachel," the earl started, reaching for her.

Rachel stepped back wildly and ran and jumped up on the bed.

The earl burst out laughing. But nothing about this seemed funny to Rachel.

"If you step down from the bed, I will explain to you what is going on. And no, we are not consummating our marriage." He whispered the last part.

Not taking her eyes off him, Rachel stepped down, but on the other side of the bed, and leaned against the wall.

"I didn't want to discuss this downstairs with the staff around."

"Of course not," Rachel muttered. She stayed put, letting the wall support her. The earl stepped forward. She slid another inch away from him.

"Rachel, no matter what happens over these next three months, I want you to be assured that I would never cause you physical harm," he said. She did not miss the pleading look in his eyes.

Cautiously, she came around and sat down on the chaise in front of the fireplace.

"I didn't know your room was on the other side of that door," she said, looking down and fingering the sash of her robe.

"I'm sorry; I thought you knew," he said.

She looked up to him, bewildered. "How would I know that? Your ways are diffcrent than mine." The house she'd grown up in was a three-bedroom ranch, and her parents still shared the same bed in one room.

Thomas had taken a seat next to her. "I suppose you don't quite 'get' any of this."

She relaxed a bit. "If I were married, I certainly wouldn't want separate rooms or even adjoining rooms. I'd want to share the bed with my man. Every night."

An unsettled look passed over the earl's face. They were both quiet for a moment. Rachel was trying not to react to sitting in close proximity to a very handsome man while they both wore their pajamas. "Surreal" didn't begin to cover it. Rachel spoke first. "And you are here because?"

He sighed, leaned forward, and rested his elbows on his thighs. "I have staff. And they will talk. It's just the nature of the beast. My plan was to spend two nights a week in here so it would put to rest any rumors that our marriage is anything but aboveboard. It's also to protect you from the gossip mill. It's for appearances' sake."

Staring at her hands in her lap, she said softly, "That's very gallant."

He shrugged. And then he looked at her more closely, his eyes narrowing. Shy, she looked away. "Are you all right?"

Embarrassed, she admitted, "I'm just a little homesick."

Concern flooded his features, softening them. "Is there anything I can do?"

She forced a smile and shook her head. Time to change the topic of conversation, she thought. She looked around the room, and her eyes landed on the queen-sized bed. "Where were you planning on sleeping?"

He patted the cushion of the chaise. "Right here. This used to be my mother's room, and when I was a boy, I fell asleep here many a time in the evening before bed."

She was warmed by this memory of his youth, and something touched her about the fact that he'd chosen to share it with her. "Would you stay all night?"

He nodded. "Yes, I'm afraid so. But I do work from home most of the time, and I'm downstairs by seven. Plus, I am away in Dublin one or two nights a week. I know this is an imposition, but I ask you to humor me. Besides, it would only be two nights a week."

Rachel studied him for a moment. His clean-shaven looks and posh accent were proving to be a heady experience, one she hadn't counted on. She looked at him evenly, and with a wry smile said, "Well, we are newlyweds. You better make it every night."

He burst out laughing.

By the time Rachel woke up the next morning, the earl was gone from her room. The previous night, she'd lain awake for a long time, acutely aware of his male presence not more than ten feet from her. He'd been quiet and said nothing. The only noise was his shifting on the chaise a few times, attempting to get comfortable. For a small child, the chaise had probably been cozy, but for an adult male well over six feet, it had to be awkward. Rachel was kind, but she wasn't kind enough to invite him to join her in her bed. That would only lead to trouble. And married or not, it was the kind of trouble she was not looking for. Besides, unless a man had her heart, he would not have her bed. Once she'd heard the rhythmic, light snore begin, confirming that he was asleep, she relaxed and soon drifted off.

She showered and dressed, thinking she'd head downstairs and explore the manor. There wasn't much for her to do, and she wasn't used to being a lady of leisure. Prior to her departure from New York, she'd asked her boss if she could work on some projects from the manor, but he had told her to take some time off for herself and that the work would be there when she returned in January. She had never had extended time off before, and she wondered what she would do with herself. Hopefully, she wouldn't grow bored.

Heading downstairs to breakfast, she ran into Mrs. Brennan.

"Will ye be having breakfast now, Lady Glenbourne?" the housekeeper asked. She glanced at her watch, noted the time, and made a small facial tic of disapproval. Her graying, blonde hair was pulled severely back into a French twist.

"Yes, please," Rachel said.

"Lord Glenbourne has asked me to go over your breakfast and lunch preferences before the day is out."

"That's fine, Mrs. Brennan. Maybe sometime after breakfast," Rachel said.

"Very well," the housekeeper said and left Rachel alone.

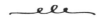

"Lord Glenbourne? Lord Glenbourne?"

Thomas's head snapped up. His secretary, Mrs. Maher, approached his desk.

"Mrs. Maher, welcome back," he said, smiling, trying to cover up the fact that he had been lost in his thoughts. Basically, thoughts about sleeping in Rachel's room. His new wife was proving to be a distraction, and he hadn't counted on that. The only cure for that was to throw himself into his work. Luckily, the company he worked for was in the midst of a major merger, and there was plenty of work to focus on.

His secretary smiled. Her salt-and-pepper hair was worn short and neat. She was a petite woman who barely reached five feet tall. But what she lacked in stature, she more than made up for in efficiency and pleasantness. She'd been with the earl since he'd decided to work three days a week from the manor. They worked well together.

"Now what's this I hear, you've gone and gotten married?" she asked, eying him suspiciously.

"It's true." He smiled.

She regarded him for a moment. "How did this come about?"

"It was a spur-of-the-moment thing," he replied.

"It must have been." Her eyes narrowed. "I didn't even know you were seeing anyone."

If his secretary kept up this line of enquiry, then all bets would be off. Mrs. Maher was extremely thorough. And she liked to get to the bottom of things.

He shrugged. "You know I don't mix business with pleasure." Before she could ask more questions, he changed the subject. "How was your day off?"

"Wonderful. Had the grandchildren all day," she replied. She tapped a varnished nail on his desk and asked, "Will I get to meet the new Lady Glenbourne soon?"

"Of course," he said. "Probably at some point today."

"I'm looking forward to it," she said, studying him intently. She slipped out of the room, and Thomas breathed a sigh of relief.

Rachel finished her meal but did not leave the breakfast room right away. The room itself called to her. She wanted to look at everything. Up close. Stepping up to the wall, she brushed the tips of her fingers along the wallpaper. Silk. It was a vibrant garden scene with hummingbirds and trees in rich colors. It was absolutely luxurious. There were paintings of still lifes on the walls. She leaned into one painting in particular, loving the old look of it, and read the scribble in the corner: *Cezanne.* She raised her eyebrows.

She studied the sideboards, impressed with their ornate details, but was glad that she didn't have to move them or dust them. If she were truly the earl's wife, she would have opened every drawer and cabinet door. But she was only a short-term guest, therefore restraint was called for.

Satisfied, she headed out of the room for further discovery. Rachel wasn't used to all this endless free time. Since high school, she had always worked. And because she worked so much, her downtime was spent at home, reading.

From there, she explored the next room, opening the door and peeking in. It was a room that demanded further investigation, and she stepped in and closed the heavy door behind her. The ballroom. It was a long room with a row of arcaded windows overlooking the lawns and gardens. Heavy crystal chandeliers hung from the vaulted ceiling. There was a parquet floor, and the walls were done up in gilt with painted murals of beautiful women in overflowing gowns, dancing away with handsome, tuxedoed men. Sunlight bloomed in the room, and Rachel saw sadly that it was a room that was not used. All the furniture was hidden under dustcovers. She went to the corner, lifted up the cover on the grand piano, and let out a little gasp at the sight of it. It was a gilded grand piano with painted scenes running around the sides of it. It was the most stunning piece of furniture Rachel had ever seen. And there it was, all covered up. *What a shame,* she thought, shaking her head.

She gave the room one last wistful look before exiting and closing the door behind her. She wandered down the gallery, taking in all the earl's ancestors, assuming from their lack of smiles they'd been a serious lot.

At the end of the gallery was a floor-to-ceiling window. She stood there gazing out at the view of the gently sloping, lush, green lawns and the thick copse of woods just beyond. She promised herself she'd go for a walk later to get some fresh air.

She opened the door at the end of the gallery, stepped inside, and gasped.

The library.

Rachel Parker thought she'd died and gone to heaven.

It was the most magnificent room she had ever been in. It was a two-story room with double-story windows on one wall looking out over the sprawling gardens. On the opposite wall, the bookshelves ran the height of the two floors. There was a winding oak staircase leading to the top gallery of books. Comfortable seating had been arranged in a semi-circular fashion in front of the windows. A large fireplace dominated a side wall, but there was no fire in the hearth, and the room was cool.

She must have stood there for a good five minutes, simply absorbing the place. It was like a dream come true. Eventually, she managed to get over her awe, put one foot in front of the other, and walk over to the first set of shelves. She ran her fingers along the bindings of the books. She pulled a copy of *Jane Eyre* from the shelf. With cautious fingers, she opened it and began to turn the pages one by one, reveling in the feel of the old book. It was a first edition. Without moving, Rachel flipped to the first page and started reading. She was so engrossed in the book that she did not hear the door open.

"There you are, Lady Glenbourne. I've been looking all over for you," Mrs. Brennan said.

Rachel was so startled that she dropped the book and bent over quickly to pick it up, but not before she saw the disapproving look on the housekeeper's face.

"It's a long-standing rule of the household that this room is to remain off-limits to anyone but the earl himself," she said.

"Oh, I did not know that," Rachel said, clutching the book to her chest.

Mrs. Brennan gave her a tight smile. "Now you do."

"What did you need me for?" Rachel asked.

"We were to go over your daily breakfast and lunch menu," the housekeeper reminded her.

"Oh, yes, of course," Rachel said. She followed Mrs. Brennan out of the room, carrying the book. She'd finish reading it in her room.

The housekeeper stopped in the doorway and nodded to the book in Rachel's hand. "No books are to be removed from the library."

"I'll bring it back," Rachel said. "I was going to finish reading it in my room." Mrs. Brennan shook her head. "That's not a good idea."

Rather than argue with her, Rachel simply replaced the book on the shelf where she had gotten it.

As they left the room, Mrs. Brennan said, "I know you're the new countess, but you'll learn our ways here at the manor."

When she turned her back, Rachel couldn't help but make a face at her. She hoped there was either a bookstore or a library in the village.

CHAPTER SIX

M RS. BRENNAN PROVED TO be efficient. First, she asked what Rachel's preferences were for breakfast and lunch.

When Rachel told her she'd prefer avocado on toast for breakfast, the housekeeper replied with a sniff, "What about porridge?"

Rachel made a face. "Yuck. It reminds me of wallpaper paste."

The other woman straightened her shoulders and said, "It's a good, hearty breakfast and will keep you going for the day."

"I'm sure it is for some, but not for me," Rachel said, standing her ground. "Avocado on toast, please."

"What about lunch then, Lady Glenbourne?" Mrs. Brennan asked, not lifting her eyes from her piece of paper.

"Salad and fruit are fine," Rachel answered.

Mrs. Brennan put down her pen and stared at Rachel. "You'll need to eat something other than fruit and salad for lunch if you plan on having babies."

Rachel blushed but she replied, "Mrs. Brennan, I'd advise you to refrain in future from making judgements on my personal choices."

The housekeeper's face turned the color of puce and without looking at Rachel, she said, "Very well, Lady Glenbourne."

There was a loaded silence between them before Mrs. Brennan asked, "And what would be your beverage of choice for breakfast and lunch?"

"Coffee for breakfast and tea and water for lunch," Rachel said. As the housekeeper marked things down on her paper, Rachel asked. "Is that all, Mrs. Brennan?"

"For now, it is," the housekeeper replied.

Without another word, Rachel stood from the table and exited the room, grateful that she only had to put up with that woman for three months.

She was no sooner out of the room when she was intercepted by a woman in her fifties.

"Ah, Lady Glenbourne, I've been looking for you," the woman said.

After her meeting with the housekeeper, Rachel remained a little wary. But the woman with the neat, short hair was smiling, and there was warmth in her eyes, so Rachel relaxed a bit.

The woman extended her hand. "I'm Ann Maher, Lord Glenbourne's secretary."

Rachel shook it and smiled. "It's nice to meet you."

"Let me show you where my office is, in case you should ever need anything."

As they walked along the gallery toward the front of the manor, Mrs. Maher chatted.

"What do you think of Ireland so far?"

"I love it. The scenery is gorgeous," Rachel said.

Mrs. Maher smiled. "That's because of all the rain we get, which you'll have to get accustomed to."

"I like rain," Rachel said. And she did. It helped her sleep. Rainy days were treats, because it meant she could curl up with a good book in a comfy chair.

The secretary laughed. "Then you've come to the right place."

Mrs. Maher's office was next to Thomas's study. It was a large space with a desk at one end. There were filing cabinets, a printer, and a desktop computer on the credenza behind her desk.

They stepped inside her office and stood there for a few moments. "This is where you will usually find me. If you should have any questions about anything at all, like questions about the staff or even where the nearest chemist is, please don't hesitate to ask."

"Thank you," Rachel said.

"And another thing," Mrs. Maher said, then paused and looked around. She lowered her voice. "Don't let Mrs. Brennan push you around."

"So noted," Rachel said.

Mrs. Maher smiled again. "You know, I can't tell you how happy I am that Lord Glenbourne has married. And I can tell already that he made an excellent choice."

Rachel didn't know what to say. But a response wasn't necessary, as the secretary continued talking.

"He works too much. If it wasn't for going up to the main office in Dublin a few days a week, he'd live like a hermit. I'm sure you'll be a breath of fresh air for this place.""I hope so," Rachel said weakly, wondering what the woman would think of her in three months when she left.

"Again, Lady Glenbourne, if you need any assistance at all with anything, please don't hesitate to ask," she said sincerely.

"Thank you, I appreciate that," Rachel said. "And call me Rachel."

"Whatever you say, Lady Glenbourne," Mrs. Maher said with a wink.

Gah.

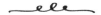

By the end of her first week at the manor, Rachel was bored. She had investigated the manor as much as she could. There were three wings not in use, and she no longer had the desire to lift dustcovers or open drapes. The amount of antiques and paintings and fine pieces had begun to overwhelm her. The obvious wealth of the Glenbournes was staggering. Plus, she was beginning to find the manor claustrophobic. For such a grand place, it was too quiet and stuffy. The staff were always around, but there was no chat and with her, they were always circumspect. There was always a nod, followed by a "Ma'am" or a "Lady Glenbourne." Once in a while, she'd hear chatter from a far-off room or filtering from the back hall, or there would be the sound of a phone ringing or the printer going from Mrs. Maher's office. But other than that, the place was as quiet as a tomb.

When Thomas wasn't in Dublin, he worked all day in his study with the door closed. Not wanting to bother him, she was left to her own devices. He did join her for lunch during the day, and she found it soon became the highlight of her day, if only to talk to another human being.

She had spoken to her family a few times that week, and she and Amy emailed back and forth. Amy kept her up-to-date regarding Brian, her children, her meetings with the architect and the project supervisor. Everything was moving along nicely.

Rachel grabbed her purse, headed out the bedroom door, and dashed down the stairs. You wouldn't want to get to the bottom of the staircase, remember that you'd forgotten something, and have to run all the way back up to your room to get it, she thought. She wondered if there was an elevator in the place but somehow, she doubted it.

She saw no one on the way out. At first, she thought she might like to walk to the village, but it would take a while to walk out of the estate, and if she did purchase something, it would be a cumbersome walk back. A walk around the estate would be lovely, but better suited to another time.

The day was sunny and dry. The blue sky held the slightest wisps of clouds, but there had been no forecast of rain. Despite it being October, the trees were still lush with leaves. She noted that some of the leaves on the sycamore trees were colored a burnt orange, reminding her that autumn had definitely arrived.

Once out of the estate, she drove along the main road of the village, taking in some of the quaint thatched cottages, the stone church, a small convenience store, and lots of dress shops. There certainly would be enough to choose from. People strolled along the sidewalks with cameras either in their hands or slung around their necks. Tour buses rolled expertly through the narrow streets of the village. There were no parking spots on the main street, but she saw a sign for parking and found a spot in the car park behind the bank.

After she locked the car, she slung her purse over her shoulder and headed back toward the main thoroughfare of the village.

The visitor center was her first stop. It was right in the middle of the village and was a round, one-story building with large windows. Inside, there were public restrooms, a souvenir shop, a first aid station, and a tourist office. At the back of the building was housed the village's historical society. At the information desk, she signed up to go out to the ruins of the thirteenth-century monastery located at the end of the village. Rachel had seen it as she drove in on her first day.

There was time before the bus departed, so she went through to the historical society and looked at their displays. There were old coins, an eighth-century chalice and some gold ingots, as well as other various and sundry artefacts that had been discovered locally. For a history major, it was all fascinating.

It also had a section on the relationship between the Earls of Glenbourne and the villagers down through the years. For the most part, it seemed an amiable association. The present earl's great-grandfather had allowed the villagers to walk through his land. But most importantly, Lord and Lady Glenbourne had kept their tenants from starving during the Great Famine of the nineteenth century. Rachel read everything that had been posted, and it seemed the village and the manor had almost always been on good terms.

The tour bus was small, so it could only accommodate a group of twenty or so people. Rachel sat in the back of the bus and listened to the tour guide.

The guided tour of the sprawling thirteenth-century ruins was awe-inspiring. It had once been a church and monastery. It, along with several outbuildings, now lay scattered in ruins, no roofs but only crumbling walls remained. Rachel was so impressed she couldn't help but wonder what other historic sites remained to be seen in the rest of Ireland.

Back in the village, Rachel had lunch at a little café and discovered the joys of banoffee pie: a caramel-and-banana concoction over a graham-cracker crust, topped with fresh cream. She felt relaxed and satisfied. So this was what it felt like to go traveling to other places. It was marvelous, she concluded.

After she finished her lunch, she walked along the footpath of the village, looking in shop windows, not anxious to return to the manor just yet. She went into the petrol shop and bought a few bags of candy to keep at her bedside, mostly chocolate. While there, she picked up a box of dog treats for Max. She liked how they called it a petrol station instead of a gas station.

As she strolled along, she stopped and admired the various window displays. The window of a boutique called Lady of the Manor drew her in to investigate further. The title was most appropriate. After all, she thought, she was the lady of the manor, if only for pretend.

When she opened the door and stepped across the threshold, a bell jingled. A woman not much older than herself stepped out from a back room. The place was done up in shades of cream, and a large cream-colored chandelier hung from the ceiling. Beneath the chandelier was a circular, cream, tufted-velvet couch.

"You're very welcome. Can I help you?" the saleswoman asked. Her tag said "Mags," and she wore expensive clothes, expensive makeup, and expensive perfume.

"Just browsing," Rachel said.

"Anything in particular?" the woman asked.

"I'm going to a wedding," Rachel improvised, regretting it as soon as the words had left her mouth.

"Is it a day wedding or an evening affair?"

"Day wedding. Church in the morning and a very small reception in the afternoon." It concerned Rachel that she was able to lie on demand like that, but she pushed it out of her mind.

The woman thought about this for a moment and looked Rachel up and down. "A size ten?"

Rachel nodded.

The woman went over to the wall and began to rummage through the racks of dresses, pulling items out and holding them up, looking at them and then at Rachel. Some she put back, and some she set aside.

Finally, with an armload of outfits, Mags turned to Rachel and said, "Follow me."

Rachel stepped into a luxurious dressing room and waited for the saleswoman to hang the dresses up and leave the room.

"I'll be right outside if you need anything," Mags said with a smile.

"Thank you," Rachel said. She undressed quickly and began trying on the outfits. They were all beautiful, but she finally settled on a long-sleeved, knee-skimming, navy silk dress with a wrap effect around the waist.

She opened the door wearing the blue dress, and the saleswoman nodded her approval.

At the counter, the shop woman asked, "Would you like a hat or a fascinator to complement your outfit?"

Rachel shook her head.

"Are you staying around here?"

Rachel nodded. "I'm staying at Glenbourne Manor."

The saleswoman stopped what she was doing. "Really? Are you a friend of the earl?"

Rachel laughed. "Yes, I guess you could say that."

"Will I open up an account for the manor?" she asked.

Rachel became alarmed. "Oh no. I'll pay for this myself."

Mags eyed her. "Very well then."

Rachel took the bag from her and departed from the shop. As she headed down the sidewalk, she soon became distracted by a shop with wedding dresses in the window. The sign read, "Caoimhe's Bridal Boutique." She wouldn't even begin to try to pronounce that. She stood for a bit and finally decided to go inside and have a look around. She had always hoped someday she'd try on a wedding dress, although obviously not under the current circumstances.

There were racks and racks of wedding dresses. A woman not much younger than Rachel stood on a platform with her arms spread out as a shop assistant circled her, a tape measure around her neck and pins lined up in her mouth. The girl's mother and bridesmaids oohed and aahed. The girl looked stunning in a princess-style bridal gown with a lace overlay.

"As soon as I put it on, I knew it was 'the one,'" the girl gushed.

Her mother nodded in agreement. "That's the magic of getting married. You just know."

The sales assistant looked toward Rachel and said, "I'll be with you in just a moment."

"That's fine. I'm only here to browse," Rachel explained.

The mother of the bride turned toward her and said, "Are you American?"

Rachel smiled. "I am."

"Where are you staying?"

Rachel hesitated before answering, "Glenbourne Manor."

They all stopped what they were doing to look at her.

"With the earl?" asked one of the bridesmaids.

Rachel nodded. Even the saleslady had stopped taking measurements, and the bride-to-be let her arms drop to her sides.

Rachel suspected that she had unwittingly overshared, and decided that looking at wedding dresses, no matter how innocent, could no longer be done.

"Actually, I'll come back another day," she said, and she turned and bolted out the door. She made a dash for her rental car and tucked the dress in the backseat. It was time to head back to the manor.

It was late afternoon by the time Rachel returned to the manor, and she was greeted at the door by the butler, Percy.

"The earl requests your presence in the study, Lady Glenbourne," the butler intoned.

Of all the staff, he was the hardest to read. At least with the housekeeper, she knew where she stood. But not with Percy. His face betrayed nothing. More than once, she wondered if he was capable of smiling.

Rachel let out a nervous giggle. "It sounds serious."

The butler did not reply and began to head toward the library.

"No need to take me there, I know where it is," Rachel told him, irritated with the thought of needing an escort every time she entered a room.

She knocked softly on the door to the earl's study and entered.

"You wanted to see me?" she asked.

The earl stood with his back to her, gazing out the window. Slowly, he turned around to face her, his hands folded behind his back. There was a look of thunder on his face. Rachel looked at him in confusion.

"Do you mind telling me what happened in the village today?" he asked.

Instinctively, Rachel took a step back, not liking his tone. "Nothing happened in the village. Absolutely nothing." Her voice had an edge to it that matched his.

"Can you enlighten me as to your day's activities?" he pressed.

"Not that it's any of your business—"

"It is if it concerns me," he interrupted.

"All right. First, I went to the visitors' center, then I went on the tour of the monastery ruins, then I went to lunch, then I strolled around the village, and then I went shopping for a dress," Rachel fumed, not happy at having to explain her itinerary.

"At any point, did you say we were married?" he asked.

"Of course not!" she said, annoyed. "Bixby International is under contract with you. I'm smart enough to know not to tell anyone about it."

"Well I had hoped so."

Rachel burned.

"Can you explain to me, then, why everyone in the village thinks you're my new love interest and that we're planning a wedding?"

Rachel's mouth fell open. "What are you talking about?"

The earl softened and relaxed his stance. He sighed. "One of the staff had a daughter ring her, saying there was an American in the village who was staying at Glenbourne Manor and who was buying a dress for a wedding."

Rachel could not hide the irritation in her voice. "Really? Two people asked me where I'm staying, and I told them the truth, told them that I knew you. And yes, I did go into a bridal shop to look around. Now if people jump to conclusions, there is nothing I can do about that."

It was the earl's turn to be annoyed. "It doesn't work that way here, not with my relationship with the press. I am unable to have any friends of the female persuasion without them designating it a romance."

Rachel said nothing.

"Look, I know you're not familiar yet with how things work, but please ask me in advance before you go anywhere."

Rachel laughed, but there was nothing funny in it. "Am I to be kept a prisoner here? I have to run every move I make by you before I do it?" She paused and waited for him to answer.

"I don't mean it like that, but there is a way to do these things. I am trying to beat the press at their own game." She could hear the exasperation in his voice.

Rachel threw her hands up. "I know you have a difficult relationship with the press."

"Difficult is too kind a word," he said.

Thoughts of her home, her family, and her own bed came to mind and suddenly, she didn't want to be in Ireland anymore. It wasn't lost on her that she had only arrived recently, but she would head back to New York and tell Mr. Bixby that this was one client they should pass on. It just wasn't a good project to take on. They had taken on lots of different problems in the past, but nothing like this. She knew if she did this, she ran the risk of Mr. Bixby firing her, and although she dreaded the thought of that, she'd deal with it if it happened. But then there was the biggest problem of all: she was legally married to Thomas Yates.

She rubbed her forehead and realized how tired she was. She was downright weary. "Maybe you should think about canceling the contract with Bixby International."

The earl stared at her and said nothing at first. "An agreement is an agreement. If I were to cancel the contract now, I would lose the means to fund the upkeep of the estate. I'm not going to do that."

She was about to protest, but he held up his hand. "I know how difficult it is having your every move scrutinized, Rachel. I'm sorry, but that's the way it is. I'm only asking you for a three-month commitment."

To Rachel, it might as well have been three years. But she knew he was right, and she knew that for Amy's sake, for Bixby, and even for the sake of Glenbourne Manor itself, she wasn't going to do anything to jeopardize their arrangement. "Now that we're talking about agreements and such, you yourself are in breach of contract," she huffed, folding her arms across her chest.

He frowned, his eyebrows knitting together. "How so?"

"I've been here a week today. Under contract, you were supposed to make me dinner one night a week and pay me one compliment," she said. She felt silly for having to ask, but since he was going to play hardball in regard to what happened in the village, she was going to fight back.

He snorted. "You can't be serious."

Tears stung the back of her eyes. She had been serious. "It's part of the contract."

"Again, I don't cook," he explained tightly. "And why should I have to pay you compliments when it's just a business arrangement?"

She thought for a moment and narrowed her eyes. "Because a gentleman always honors his word."

The earl breathed in deeply. He pressed his lips together until they disappeared and gave a nod. "You're right. I will see what I can do about dinner."

"Thank you. Now, what are we going to do about this morning?" she asked.

"I've given it a lot of thought. And now that the cat is out of the bag prematurely, I say we just move the press release up, because once the press gets wind of this rumor, they'll descend in no time."

Rachel looked at him. "What day are you moving it up to?"

He looked at her squarely and said, "Tomorrow morning. We'll release the press statement first thing in the morning."

And what Rachel had been trying to avoid, she now had to do: tell her parents about her marriage. As she left the study, the earl called out to her.

"Rachel?"

She turned back toward him, expectant. "Yes?"

He stood behind his desk, tapping his fingers on it. "Um, you have lovely hair."

"Thanks," she said, rolling her eyes. She closed the door behind her, thinking he was hopeless as a husband.

The following morning, it hit the papers that the Earl of Glenbourne was no longer Ireland's most eligible bachelor. A company photo of Rachel from Bixby International was on the front page with the caption, "Who's That Girl?" Another paper told all about her background and her work at Bixby International, a solutions-oriented company, which begged the question, "What Problem Did the Earl Need Solving?"

CHAPTER SEVEN

"WHAT DO YOU MEAN, you've *married* this Earl of Glencourt?" Rachel's mother's voice boomed down the phone line.

"Glenbourne," Rachel corrected.

"I don't care what it is," her mother said. Rachel knew her mother's tone too well. It indicated that she was furious with the current situation, and Rachel could hardly blame her.

There was silence, and then her mother spoke again. "Is this true?"

Rachel took a deep breath. "Yes, Mom, it is."

At first, her mother was quiet, and then she wailed, "How could you get married without us? You're our only daughter! To deny us this privilege—how could you?"

In a sense, Rachel was relieved. Her mother was more upset about missing her wedding than the fact that Rachel had just married a total stranger and was now living in a foreign country. She was more than happy not to have to get into that subject.

"I'm sorry, Mom. Things happened so fast that we didn't really have time to think," she said. That part was true. She was still trying to wrap her head around that and figure a way out of it. But the earl had promised her that he would have them divorced in no time once the three months were up.

"Never mind that now. What's done is done," her mother said. "But we're coming over there as soon as we can arrange it."

"What?" Rachel asked. That was the last thing she needed. Or wanted. Her mother descending on her and the earl. That would end up in utter chaos. She could fake her feelings and her "marriage" to those in Ireland. But to her own family? Even her mother, despite being caught up in all the trappings of the title, the manor, and the money, would eventually see through the charade. "That's not a good idea."

But it was her father she was most worried about. He was astute, and as soon as he stepped off the plane and saw her face, the ruse would be up. There was enough going on without having to tell the earl that her family was descending.

"Your father and I are eager to meet our new son-in-law," her mother explained. "Your brothers are very anxious to meet him and will come over as soon as they can get time off from work."

Rachel cringed. She could only imagine. With her being the youngest of the family and the only girl, they'd been overprotective. Back in high school, she had brought boyfriends home only twice. After they met her brothers, that had ended that. Her brothers had been merciless, and even though that had been fifteen or so years ago, something told her things hadn't changed.

"But don't worry, they'll come over as soon as they can," her mother chirped.

Rachel's heart sank. The fake marriage was taking on a life of its own. Now her family had been dragged into it. At some point, she was going to have to explain to them what was going on, and how she'd be in the market for a divorce right after Christmas. A sweat broke out on her forehead, and her stomach roiled.

"Mom, I'm not feeling well. It must have been something I ate. I feel like I'm going to throw up," Rachel said. That was the truth.

"Oh my goodness! Do you think you're pregnant?" her mother practically screamed.

"No! Definitely not!" Rachel said. Panic filled her. That's just what they needed: pregnancy rumors swirling around them. How would she explain *that* to Thomas?

"Oh, just think: if it was a boy, my grandson would be the future Earl of Glencourt," her mother said. Her glee filled the other side of the Atlantic.

"Mom, listen to me. I'm not pregnant," Rachel said firmly, not bothering to correct her on the title.

"That's disappointing," her mother said. She paused and then asked, "What are you waiting for?"

"We only just got married!" Rachel said, unable to believe that they were having this conversation.

"Well, I know how these dynastic families work; they want the heir and the spare sorted so they can get on with their lives," her mother said.

Rachel thought her mother watched too much TV.

"Okay, I've got to go. Thomas is calling me," Rachel lied.

"Let us know when we can come over," her mother said.

"Will do."

"I love you, honey."

"Me too, Mom." Rachel felt a pang of sadness at missing her mother.

The news about their marriage had been in the papers in the morning and by afternoon, the vicar had arrived.

"Reverend Gibbons, may I introduce my wife, Rachel?" Thomas said.

Rachel shook his hand and noted that the vicar was a thin, wiry man with a head of curly white hair.

"Lady Glenbourne, may I congratulate you on your marriage and say that you are very welcome here."

"Thank you, Reverend Gibbons." She smiled.

The vicar cast a side glance at Thomas. "May I also say that your marriage has taken many people by surprise, including me."

Rachel laughed. "You're not the only one."

Thomas smiled to himself. His new bride had a nice sense of humor. He wondered if that would constitute a compliment. With a gesture of his hand, he invited the vicar to sit down in the study.

"I'll get straight to the point, Lord Glenbourne," the vicar said, crossing his legs and folding his hands over his knees. It was hard to read his expression as the sunlight streamed in through the windows, casting a reflective glare on the vicar's prescription glasses. But Thomas didn't need to read his expression to know why the vicar was there. "Although I offer my most heartfelt congratulations on your marriage, I am a little disappointed that you didn't get married in the church."

This was exactly what the earl had been expecting. Everyone who was anyone would want to row in on their marriage.

"Reverend Gibbons, Rachel and I made a spontaneous decision to get married, without any thought as to how or where. All we knew was we wanted to get married right away—"

The vicar looked over at Rachel. "Is there a child on the way that would have pressed you to marry so quickly?"

"No!" Rachel said, aghast.

The vicar backpedaled. "Excuse me, Lady Glenbourne. I meant no disrespect. Babies are always welcome."

"None taken," Rachel said, giving the man of the cloth a reassuring smile.

Reverend Gibbons looked to Thomas. "Do you plan on a church wedding?"

Both Rachel and the vicar waited for his answer.

Thomas had to weigh up his heritage and obligations against the business arrangement of his marriage. "We hadn't given it any thought."

With a forced smile, the vicar broke eye contact. "You haven't given it any thought," the vicar repeated, picking at an imaginary piece of lint on his trouser leg. "Unfortunately, that is the sign of the times. However, might I point out to you, Lord Glenbourne, that as long as there have been Earls of Glenbourne, all the earls have married their brides in the chapel on the estate."

Thomas knew this, and that was why he had to tread delicately. "I perfectly understand my heritage and my obligations, to it and because of it."

"Well, Lord Glenbourne, I'm relieved to hear that," the vicar said. He turned to Rachel. "And you, Lady Glenbourne, would you like a church wedding?"

The earl resented him for putting Rachel on the spot. When she seemed to be struggling with the answer, the vicar asked, "I thought all women were partial to a big church wedding."

Rachel laughed and scratched her forehead. "That may be true for some, but I can assure you that a big wedding would not be for me."

Well played, Rachel.

Reverend Gibbons seemed surprised by this admission. "Really? Indeed, you are a rare breed."

Thomas spoke up. "Yes, she is, and that's one of the things that drew me to her." He watched with interest as her face softened. "My wife is reserved and wouldn't be flamboyant in any way, shape, or form."

"I see." The vicar smiled, nodding his head in approval. "How refreshing in this generation of endless self-promotion on social media."

"Exactly," Thomas agreed. He winked at Rachel. "Now, Reverend Gibbons, can I interest you in a slice of apple tart? I know how fond you are of Mrs. Shortt's apple tart and I know for a fact she made one today."

"That would be lovely, Lord Glenbourne."

"Let's have some tea, and in the meantime, leave the subject of a wedding in the chapel with my wife and me, and we'll get back to you," Thomas said, closing the topic of discussion.

Later, after the vicar left, Thomas found himself in the kitchen with Mrs. Shortt. The cook was anything but short. In fact, she was a tall, thin woman with dark hair and a long nose.

"Mrs. Shortt, you're free to take the rest of the day off," he said.

She'd been in the middle of making a fruitcake, something Thomas was fond of. Her hand stopped mixing the batter, and she looked up at him in confusion.

"Take the rest of the day off? But why?" she asked.

"Because there won't be a need for you to cook a dinner for Lady Glenbourne and me tonight," he explained.

"Are you going out for a meal?" she asked. She folded raisins, currants, and orange peel into the batter.

He shook his head, resentful of his new wife at having to explain to his cook that he needed to use her kitchen. "Actually, I was going to try to cook something myself." He knew his voice sounded unconvincing.

"You?" Mrs. Shortt said with a slight smile. She stopped stirring the batter, took the spoon out, and laid it to rest on the table. Coming out from behind the large farmhouse table, she wiped her hands on her apron. "What are you planning on cooking?" She paused and then looked at him. "Excuse me, Lord Glenbourne, but do you even know how to cook?"

He shook his head slowly. "I just thought it might be something nice to do."

Mrs. Shortt broke into a long, generous smile. "Ah, to be newly married. I remember it well. Just always wanting to do nice things for the other."

He smiled in response. "That's exactly it. I thought it might be a little less formal if I cooked a meal."

"Seeing as how you don't know how to cook, it will certainly be informal!" She laughed.

He laughed with her.

"Come on, let's see what we can come up with," she said.

He started to follow her toward the pantry, and she glanced over her shoulder and asked, "You don't mind me helping you out a bit, Lord Glenbourne?"

He shook his head and laughed. "Not at all, Mrs. Shortt. I need all the help I can get."

As Rachel sat down at the dining-room table, to the right of Thomas's chair, he was just walking through the door with a soup tureen in his hands. Granted, he had used a packet soup mix, but Mrs. Shortt had told him that putting it in the tureen would dress it up a bit. She'd suggested sandwiches to be served with the soup. She'd advised that Lady Glenbourne might be more partial to a grilled cheese sandwich, which was the American way, rather than a toasted cheese sandwich, which was the Irish way. She'd told him how to butter both sides of the bread and fry it up until it was golden brown. She'd said to use the mature red cheddar cheese he'd find in the stainless-steel, American-style refrigerator. And to add a thin slice of tomato to liven it up.

He'd reassured her that he was capable of doing all of this, and Mrs. Shortt had removed her apron and hung it up on a hook on the side wall. Beaming, she was still muttering about romance and love when she'd departed the kitchen.

He ladled soup from the tureen into two bowls and set the first one in front of Rachel. He hoped she wasn't expecting an extravagant meal like the ones Mrs. Shortt prepared for them. Ever a solicitor at heart, he had his arguments ready for any objections she should put forth.

"Did you make this?" she asked, looking up at him.

He nodded. "I did." He handed her a plated grilled cheese sandwich. "Look, if you're expecting a three-course meal—"

She shook her head and smiled. "No, it's perfect."

Thinking she would surely find fault; he was at a loss at her statement. Saying nothing more, he sat down next to her and began eating his meal. He was so used to being alone that—she was right—it was awkward. He didn't really know what to say to her. What was he supposed to say? Ask her what her favorite color was? Was that how people got to know one another? It might just be easier to hand her a questionnaire to fill out. Shouldn't getting to know someone be a gradual unfolding of events and information?

She bit into her sandwich and chewed thoughtfully. "It's very good. I'm impressed."

His soup spoon hesitated at his mouth, and he looked at her. "Are you?"

She nodded. "I am, because you said you didn't know how to cook."

"I don't."

"You've managed this," she said.

He nodded.

"Well, I appreciate the effort," she said.

It was more than he'd expected. He finished his soup and decided to change gears. "How are you finding it? Living at the manor, I mean?" he asked.

"I'm surprised that, for a place so big, it's so quiet," she remarked. "It's so different from what I'm used to that it may take a bit to adjust."

He nodded, not knowing what to say.

"Was it quiet while you were growing up?" she asked.

At first, he didn't answer, as he was studying her face. She wore a bit of mascara, which highlighted her eyes, and a matte peach lipstick that made her complexion seem even creamier. Finding his voice, he replied, "I didn't grow up here."

"Really?" she asked, unable to hide her surprise.

"My parents actually lived in Dublin when I was a child," he explained.

"Did you like living in Dublin?"

He shook his head. "I spent most of my time in boarding school, and my holidays were spent here with my grandfather." He hadn't had the happiest of childhoods; he only spent time with his parents here when they came for the holidays. And every summer had been spent at the manor. Those months every year had been the happy, magical times. His grandfather, the 10th Earl of Glenbourne, had been a wonderful grandparent. They had spent a lot of time together. He'd died when Thomas was seventeen, and it was a death Thomas had never truly recovered from. He still missed his grandfather to this day.

"Is that why you decided to come and live here full time?" she asked.

He nodded, shifting in his seat. They were veering into private territory. Even though she was his wife, she really wasn't. "This place was always full of happy memories for me."

Before she could respond, he stood up, lifting their plates. "I didn't make a dessert or anything, but I'm sure there's some ice cream in the kitchen. I'll be right back."

By the middle of October, the rain had started, and to Rachel, it seemed at times that it would never stop. A trip to the library was in order, she concluded. There was nothing better than curling up with a good book on a rainy day. She wasn't going to let a little downpour deter her. The dog, Max, stood waiting for her at the front door. She pulled a treat from her pocket and held out her hand. With a wet tongue, he helped himself. She patted the dog's head. "Now, Max, you can't come with me. But I'll be back in a bit, and then if it stops raining, we'll go for a walk. If not, we'll find a nice fire to sit by. You're a good dog."

The dog gave a little whine, and she massaged his ears and blew him a kiss.

She grabbed an umbrella from the stand in the hallway and headed out to the village.

Even on a damp, dreary day, the village still retained its charm. The thatched cottages added a splash of color to the overall gray and dark atmosphere. As she rounded the corner of a row of terraced buildings, a middle-aged man wearing a white apron rolled a beer barrel out of a pub and placed it in the street with others, for collection.

He stood up, wiping his hands on his apron, and gave her a nod, "Countess."

She blushed and smiled. Even if she and Thomas were truly married, she'd never get used to the title. "Good morning."

He responded with a generous smile. "Don't catch your cold, now." He nodded again and disappeared inside.

Rachel strolled in the direction of the library, holding the umbrella firmly over her head. The library was a small, Tudor-style building at the edge of the village. The rain spattered down on top of it, and she listened as cars drove by, splashing rain up onto the sidewalk, or the footpath, as they called it in Ireland. She moved farther away from the street, not wanting to get wet.

Outside the library doors, she shook her umbrella free from water, closed it, and set it against the wall. She smoothed her hair back, opened the door, and walked in, breathing in the quiet and the smell of books and paper. She closed her eyes and sighed. Heaven.

In the outer vestibule, the day's newspapers lay scattered about the tables. A few elderly men were seated in chairs, gathered around the tables perusing the papers. Some lowered their papers, looked up from their reading, and made eye contact. She smiled, and most of them nodded in return.

Entering the main room, she found two librarians seated behind the main desk. She approached.

"Can I help you?" asked the one with the short hair and glasses.

"I'd like to apply for a library card," Rachel said.

"Of course," the woman said. She pulled an application form from a pile and handed it, along with a pen, to Rachel.

Rachel filled out the form and handed it back to the librarian.

The woman glanced over it and looked up at Rachel. "Lady Glenbourne, would you care to browse? Your card will be ready by the time you leave."

Rachel smiled. "I would love to."

After a while, she stacked her books on the counter and was glad she'd remembered to bring a canvas bag. As the librarian checked out her books, Rachel glanced around the place.

There was a lot of activity going on in the library. There were what appeared to be secondary students hanging up paintings along the library's wall. She noted their uniforms with interest. They were navy blue with gold and red. The boys wore navy trousers with navy V-neck pullovers over white shirts and navy-and-red-striped ties. On their pullovers was the crest of the school in a navy badge with red and gold. The girls' uniforms were the same on top, with the pullovers, shirts, and ties, but they wore skirts that went to their ankles. Rachel found that curious. They appeared to be having good fun.

The librarian noted Rachel's interest and said, "Those are our transition-year students from the secondary school."

"Transition year?" Rachel questioned.

"Yes. What you might call a gap year?" The librarian explained. "The students have the option to take a break after the third year. It's a year that's spent gaining some work experience, doing activities, a bit of traveling, and community work. It's very successful here."

"I would have loved an opportunity like that when I was in high school," Rachel remarked.

"We are having a showing of local artists and their works next week, and the students are running it."

"That sounds wonderful," Rachel said.

"Would you like to come?" the librarian asked.

Rachel hesitated for a moment, but then said, "I'd love to."

The librarian handed her a glossy postcard. "Here are the details. The students designed the posters and the postcards themselves."

Rachel did not miss the pride in the librarian's voice. She glanced at the postcard, noting the date and time, and said, "I'll mark this down in my diary. I look forward to it." She tucked it, along with her books, into her canvas bag.

"I'm Marian, by the way," the librarian said.

Rachel nodded. "I'm Rachel."

"It's nice to meet you, Lady Glenbourne," Marian said with a smile.

Once checked out, Rachel said goodbye and headed outside. She looked up to the sky; it had brightened a bit, and the rain had stopped. She grabbed her umbrella and headed back to her car, stopping only to pick up a few bags of candy. And more dog treats.

CHAPTER EIGHT

T HOMAS HAD JUST SAT down for breakfast when Rachel arrived. He was glad for the company. She usually didn't join him for breakfast, as she didn't get up as early as he did. The past few nights, she had stayed up late in bed, reading her book with a book light and eating candy. Amused, he had listened from his uncomfortable spot on the chaise. His back was beginning to bother him, and he wondered if he should go back to sleeping in his own bed in his own room a couple of nights a week. But he was in no hurry to leave her room, which surprised him. He was grateful for those few minutes alone in the morning, as he liked to watch her sleep. She looked so peaceful.

"Good morning, Rachel," he said, unfolding his napkin.

"Good morning, Thomas," she said.

He wondered if she was ever in a bad mood. If she was, he hadn't witnessed it. She was homesick; he had copped on to that. He had caught her crying twice, and each time she'd just shake her head and say, "missing my family" or, "missing home." It bothered him that she couldn't seem to shake it.

She'd been there almost three weeks. But fair play to her, she kept herself busy. She was always going off to the village or walking the grounds of the manor. He had seen her and Max strolling the grounds from the windows in his study. The dog, once so loyal to him, had taken an immediate shine to Rachel. In the past week, he'd come down in the morning with Max waiting at the base of the staircase. The only difference was, he no longer followed him around, instead choosing to wait at the bottom of the stairs until Rachel came down. One morning, he'd heard the dog whining, and he'd poked his head out and seen his great big wolfhound whining and pacing as Rachel made her way down the staircase. It was only when she reached the bottom of the stairs and lavished attention on him, pulling a dog treat from her pocket, that the dog relaxed. Then he'd watched as the dog trotted after Rachel, his tail wagging happily. *Traitor,* Thomas had thought.

Percy set a silver tray to his right. The morning newspapers lay on top of it.

A quick glance showed a photo of Rachel on the front page. Curious, the earl picked up the top paper and unfolded it. The headline read, "Honeymoon for One," and there were pictures of Rachel in the village, leaving the library with a bag of books and strolling around town. The sub headline was, "What bride has time to read? Is the earl not doing his job?" The insinuation that there was something wrong with his manhood irritated him. Had they nothing better to do? He looked again at the photo, wondering why Rachel went to the village library when the manor had a perfectly good library.

"May I see a section?" Rachel asked, sitting down next to him with her breakfast on her plate. "Anything but the sports section."

Without a word, he handed her the front page. She bit into her toast and her eyes widened as she scanned the headlines. She set the newspaper down and looked at him.

"I am so sorry," she said. "I didn't know I was being followed."

"It's not your fault," he said. And he meant it. He had hoped with the marriage announcement the press would have gone home, but apparently not. They were off his back, but the problem was, they had now turned their attention to Rachel. And he wished they hadn't. She didn't deserve to be under such scrutiny. In his overarching desire to get the press off his back, he had inadvertently shifted the focus from him to her. He blamed himself. Rachel had gone quiet, poring over the newspapers.

"Maybe a small press conference to introduce me and answer a few questions," Rachel suggested.

"Is it necessary?"

"I'm afraid so. I don't treasure it any more than you, but we didn't expect the heightened interest surrounding our marriage," she explained. She poured herself more tea and bit into her breakfast of avocado on toast. "And we should have."

He harrumphed. "I don't even have that much interest in our marriage."

A shadow crossed Rachel's face. Apparently what he'd said had affected her, and he reminded himself to be more careful with his choice of words.

"Needs must and all that."

He groaned. "I'm a busy man."

"I understand that, but there are a few other things as well. We need to cover our story about how we met. That will be one of the first questions asked."

"Really?" he asked.

She nodded and said, "When was the last time you were in the States?"

He thought for a moment. "About nine months ago. January. I went over for a conference in New York for two weeks."

Rachel smiled. "That's perfect. We'll say we met then and prepare to be asked where and how, and we'll say we prefer to keep that private, as that first meeting remains precious to us. We kept in touch through emails, and a strong friendship developed. Our schedules did not allow for a second visit until September, and we decided we couldn't live without one another and got married!" She clapped her hands in excitement.

"You should have been a writer," the earl said.

"Nope, I'm happy with my job," she said.

Thomas finished his orange juice. "It sounds like you've got this all sorted out—the press release, that is," he said.

"That's my job," she said.

"Any other suggestions?" he asked.

"That we go into the village together, even if it's just to take a stroll or get a cup of coffee, something simple that a newly married couple would do," she suggested.

He seemed to ponder this and decided spending time with her was not a bad thing. "Okay." As an afterthought, he added, "Sammy has invited us to dinner with him and Trish. That might be a 'couple' thing to do."

She nodded but looked hesitant.

"Is that all right?"

Rachel nodded quickly. "Of course it is."

"Then I'll ring him and tell him to make arrangements."

The press conference took place on the steps of Glenbourne Manor. Rachel wore the navy silk dress she'd purchased, and Thomas was dressed in business casual: shirt, jacket, and trousers, but no tie. He sensed Rachel's nervousness and stepped a bit closer to her side in a protective manner. He hated to have to put her through this, but he reminded himself that it was her job, so to speak. Still, he was pretty certain she hadn't been under such scrutiny in the States. He noted all the major Irish newspapers were present, as well as the local ones and some he didn't recognize.

"Can you tell us where you first met?" asked a middle-aged woman in the front row.

The earl took this one. "I was in New York on business, and we met by chance at the Metropolitan Museum of Art." For effect, he glanced at Rachel, and she responded with a smile.

"Was it love at first sight?" someone from the back of the crowd shouted.

Thomas and Rachel exchanged a glance and smiled knowingly at one another.

"It started out as a friendship and grew into love," Rachel answered. When she spoke, they listened attentively.

"Lady Glenbourne, have you ever been to Ireland before?" someone asked.

Rachel shook her head.

"Countess Glenbourne, how do you like Ireland?"

"I love it; it's a beautiful country," she said enthusiastically.

"Do you miss the States? Do you miss your family?" asked someone in the front row.

"Yes, of course I do," she said.

Thomas did not miss the tremor in her voice. She looked a bit lost. Instinctively, he reached out and took her hand in his. He gave it a gentle squeeze, and she looked up and smiled at him. For a moment, he felt lost himself. In the broad daylight and up close and personal, he noticed her brown eyes had flecks of gold in them. He forced himself back to the task at hand and added, "Of course, we'll be visiting the States as well."

"Countess Glenbourne, do have plans to become a patron of any philanthropic causes?"

Rachel looked confused and looked up at Thomas.

"The countess has yet to decide what charity projects she'll undertake," the earl said, and added wryly, "Come on lads, we're only newly married."

A chuckle rippled through the crowd.

"Any plans for children?" asked someone. The reporters went quiet and strained to hear.

Thomas lifted an eyebrow and said, "Now, we can't tell you all our plans; we have to keep something for ourselves. And on that note, we bid you all a good day."

A flurry of questions was shouted out after them as Thomas and Rachel turned to head back into the manor. The earl did not let go of her hand until they were safely inside.

"That went well," the earl noted, once they had closed the French doors behind them.

Rachel nodded in agreement. "I think so, too. Short and sweet but just enough so they could take some pictures and ask a few questions."

"We should have a drink to celebrate," he said, walking over to the drinks cabinet. He wasn't one for drinking in the afternoon, but he felt unsettled. He wanted to blame it on the press conference, but it was holding her hand that had done it. Again, he had to remind himself that this was a business arrangement. That she had a job to do, as had he. This had been his idea. He couldn't afford to let the lines blur between them. After Christmas, when the ninety days were up, she would head back to the States, and in his head, he was already contriving the breakdown of the marriage. The term "parting amicably" came to mind, and it would be said that she missed her home, family, and country too much for it to work. He had it all worked out. In another month, they could plan her exit strategy together. Now, if only his feelings wouldn't get in the way.

The press conference had unnerved Rachel. The handholding, the earl's hand at the small of her back, and the way he'd looked at her. If it weren't a business arrangement, it would almost have felt real. To have a man look at her that way, as if he saw her and no one else . . . She reminded herself that it was all for show and not to get any notions in her head. Being in a foreign country was exotic, living at the manor was luxurious, and it would be easy to lose her head and start running away with all sorts of thoughts.

But the press conference hadn't made Rachel anxious in the same way the upcoming dinner with Sammy and Trish did. This was much more intimate. She hardly knew Sammy, and she had never met Trish. They were meeting in a restaurant in Dublin, which was a little more than an hour away. Worried over her appearance, she changed her outfit three times before settling on a block-print wrap dress, black stockings, and black knee-high boots. Minus her regular headband, she let her hair fall naturally around her shoulders. With some care, she applied smoky eyeshadow, black eyeliner, and mascara, as well as blush and lipstick. Taking one last look in the cheval mirror, she smiled at herself. Glancing at the clock, she realized she was late. Not wanting to keep Thomas waiting any longer, she grabbed her purse and coat and headed downstairs.

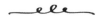

Thomas stood at the foot of the grand staircase, waiting for Rachel. He had wanted to leave ten minutes ago. He glanced at his watch again and as he did, he heard Rachel coming down the stairs.

At his side, Max began to whine and wag his tail. The earl looked at his dog and whispered, "She already has you spoiled, doesn't she?"

"I'm so sorry I'm late," she said, reaching the bottom of the stairs.

He looked up and his mouth fell open. *Who was this?*

With a laugh, she said, "I couldn't decide what to wear."

He took in every bit of her. Her thick, dark hair fell around her shoulders. The dress hugged every curve, and her long legs were cased in black leather boots with four-inch heels. He was mesmerized.

She looked at him, unsure. "Is it all right? I can change."

He shook his head slowly. "No, you look dynamite."

She rewarded him with a shy smile. "I'll count that as your compliment for the week." She slipped Max a treat.

"He's wrapped around your finger," Thomas noted, watching as the dog kept his eyes fixed on Rachel.

"He's such a lovely dog," Rachel said, patting Max's head.

Thomas could see how the dog was thriving under her devoted attention. He couldn't help but wonder, if he had married her for love, would she have devoted her attention to him? And would he have thrived too?

After a moment, she asked, "Are we ready?"

Coming back to planet Earth, Thomas said, "Yes, we are. Here, let me help you with your coat."

With his hand on the small of her back, he escorted her out to the car, gauging his reaction to her. All of a sudden, he was looking forward to dinner in Dublin. Hell, he was even looking forward to sitting next to her in the car on the ride up.

The Croydon Restaurant in Dublin had only been open a year and was owned and operated by a chef whose sole goal was to get a Michelin Star. It was the type of restaurant where people who wanted to avoid the press went for a great meal and lots of privacy. Which was why the earl had chosen it. Everything was done up in black, the lighting minimal. When they entered, they followed the maitre'd to their table, where Sammy and Trish waited.

As they walked through the restaurant, Thomas was aware of heads casually turning. It wasn't him they were looking at but his wife. Pride spread through him. Proprietarily, he placed his hand on the small of her back.

He knew Rachel was nervous; she had admitted as much on the way up. His only job tonight was to make her feel comfortable. Although they hadn't been together long, he had learned some things about his new wife. She was shy and reserved. She was also intelligent and kind.

Sammy's reaction when he saw Rachel confirmed what the earl knew: Rachel looked beautiful. The earl hugged Trish, Sammy's longtime girlfriend. Trish was not privy to the scheme. Sammy had promised he wouldn't tell her. Thomas didn't know what was taking his friend so long to marry Trish. They were so well suited to one another.

He introduced Rachel to Trish, and both women seemed friendly toward one another. He pulled Rachel's chair out for her and sat next to her. She glanced at him, and he sensed her nervousness. Reflexively, he reached out and squeezed her hand in reassurance. Besides, hadn't that been one of her conditions? Gestures of affection in public?

After the meal, Rachel and Trish paired up and headed to the ladies' room. Rachel was glad dinner was over, and it hadn't been as bad as she'd feared. Trish was as friendly as Sammy, and the conversation flowed. The other woman's easygoing manner had immediately put Rachel at ease. She was a pretty girl, petite with honey-blonde hair and blue eyes.

At the sink, they touched up their makeup.

"What's your secret?" Trish asked.

"To what?" Rachel regarded her in the mirror.

"To getting Tommy to propose to you after a very short courtship," Trish said, applying compact powder to her face. "Sammy and I have been going out for five years, and every time I bring up marriage, he bolts like a horse from the stable."

"It sounds like he's comfortable with the way things are." Rachel said.

"Oh definitely," Trish said. She pressed her lips together. "Maybe a little too much. Sometimes I think he takes me for granted."

"Have you sat down and talked to him? Told him how you feel?" Rachel asked, wiping a smudge from beneath her eye with a tissue.

Trish sighed. "I've tried, but he doesn't take it seriously.""Maybe you need to shake him up a bit," Rachel suggested.

"Maybe I do," Trish agreed.

They put their cosmetics back into their clutches and exited the restroom.

After they returned to the table, dessert was ordered.

Rachel's eyes grew wide as the waiter brought out her dessert, labeled "Chocolate Decadence."

"Oh wow, that looks good," Rachel said. "Will you share it with me?" she asked Thomas.

He smiled. "I will." He looked at Trish and said, "My wife has a sweet tooth."

Trish smiled.

Rachel looked at him questioningly.

"I've noticed the bag of candy on your bedside table," he explained.

Rachel blushed. Sammy raised an eyebrow. The earl had his arm resting along the back of her chair. Although they weren't in the same league as Sammy and Trish, Rachel thought they were making a good impression as a newly married couple.

"I suppose you got that invitation to Teddy Stabler's next month?" Sammy asked.

"I did," the earl said glumly. Rachel looked at him.

"Are you going?" Trish asked Rachel.

Caught on the back foot, Rachel stuttered, but Thomas intervened. "I'd forgotten to mention it to her. It's a party at the Stabler estate in Kildare. As it's for a children's charity, we will have to go." He looked apologetically at Rachel.

"I don't mind," Rachel said.

Trish leaned over the table and whispered to Rachel, "Just a word of advice, Rachel. Don't ever be alone in a room with Teddy Stabler. He has a bad rep with women."

Rachel tucked that piece of information away for future reference.

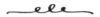

The dinner with friends had left them both in good humor. Thomas decided to seize on that and get to the bottom of something. It bothered him that Rachel borrowed books from the village library and yet never used the one at the manor. It would be one thing if she read contemporary fiction, but he had eyed her books on her bedside table and seen they were the classics, most of which he was sure were right downstairs in his own home.

As they got ready for bed, she went about the room doing last-minute things. She laid out her clothes for the following morning. Absentmindedly, she brushed her hair as she puttered around the room. The brushing of her hair he found mesmerizing, and he loved to watch her do it. But more than that, he would have loved to do it for her. She had beautiful hair. She sat on her side of the bed and lifted up the legs of her pajama bottoms to rub cream into her legs. He found himself wanting to do that for her too. This simple, daily routine of hers he found enchanting. Women were mysterious, wonderful creatures.

In the beginning, she'd done all these things behind the closed door of the bathroom, but as time went on, she seemed to take no notice of him in her bedroom and just got on with things. What did that say about him if she no longer took notice of him in her bedroom?

Rachel Parker was a curious creature, and he had to admit to being entranced.

As she settled in the bed, he tried to make himself comfortable on the chaise.

"Can I ask you something, Rachel?" he asked, watching her pull the blankets up to her shoulders. She had a thing about that too; she didn't like her shoulders uncovered when she slept.

"Sure, anything." She smiled. Then she clarified with a laugh, "Well, almost anything."

"I assure you, it's nothing personal," he said. "But I am curious about one thing."

"And what is that?" She looked over at him with her doe eyes.

"Why do you never use the library here at the manor?"

There was a look of surprise on her face.

"I mean, I see you bringing all these books back from the library in the village, and I can't help but wonder why you don't look through the library here.""Because it's off-limits," she replied.

Confused, he laughed. "What?"

"The room is off-limits, and the books are not allowed to leave the room," she explained. There was a strange look on her face, as if she expected him to know that.

"Where on earth did you get that idea from?"

"Mrs. Brennan. She found me in there one day and told me that I wasn't allowed to be there, and that I couldn't take any books out of the room," she said matter-of-factly. Rachel didn't seem offended.

But he was. "Not allowed?" he repeated. Anger coursed through him. Sometimes he wondered who was lord of the manor around here.

"Oh, Thomas, don't be mad," Rachel said quickly. "I promise, I didn't take any books out of the room. I know how priceless they are."

Why would she think he would get angry about removing books from the library? What kind of image was he projecting to her? Obviously, the wrong one. That changed now.

He jumped up from the chaise, grabbed his bathrobe, and pulled it on. Rachel sat up. He picked up her robe and walked around to her side of the bed. "Come on, Rachel. Come with me." He held her bathrobe open for her.

"Now?" she asked.

He nodded. "Please.""But where are we going?" she asked, slowly sliding her feet out from under the duvet.

"You'll see."

Hesitantly, she slipped on the robe and tied the sash around her waist.

He did not miss the look of surprise when he took her by the hand and led her out of the bedroom.

She protested. "But we're in our pajamas. What if the staff sees us?"

"Who cares? Besides, they've either gone to bed or gone home."

He pulled her behind him, padding quickly down the hall in his slippers and then down the grand staircase. When he arrived at the end of the gallery, he threw open the door to the library and pulled her in with him, flipping on the lights. The wood trim gleamed under all the amber lighting, and Rachel's eyes widened in delight.

He did not let go of her hand. Rachel looked at him in confusion.

"Do you like this room?" he asked, looking around at it himself.

She nodded and said quietly, "It's my favorite room in the manor."

He looked back at her, his eyes not leaving her face. "Rachel, this room is yours. This is my gift to you. Nothing in this house is off-limits to you." Including himself, he wanted to add, but he bit his tongue.

Nothing could have surprised him more than when she flung her arms around his neck and hugged him. He saw the look of joy on her face at his gift. When she hugged him, pressing her body against his, he was certain that the look on his face matched hers.

They headed back upstairs. She was happy, and so was he. Once the lights went out, Thomas lay back on the chaise, his hands folded behind his head, and stared at the ceiling. In his mind, he replayed the expression on her face when he had "given" her the library. It was one of pure joy. He smiled to himself. He looked over at her in the dark. She was on her side, and from the rise and fall of her body, he could tell she was already asleep. He stood up from the chaise and walked over to her. Gently, he pulled the blanket up and tucked it around her shoulder.

"Sleep well, my wife," he whispered, wishing he could lay a kiss on her shoulder.

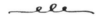

"You wish to see me, Lord Glenbourne?" Mrs. Brennan asked, entering the study.

Thomas, busy with work, looked up from his laptop.

"Yes, I do," he said, removing his reading glasses and laying them down on his desk. He sat back in the chair. "I just want to review a few things with you, because there seems to be a misunderstanding."

The housekeeper visibly stiffened. She had been with their family since his father's time, and he wondered if she was ever going to retire.

"I can assure you, my lord, there is no misunderstanding on anything," she said.

"That remains to be seen," he replied. "I want to clarify something in relation to Lady Glenbourne."

Mrs. Brennan remained silent, but her lips were pursed in a grim line.

"Lady Glenbourne is free to use any room in the manor as she likes. And that includes the library. What she does in the library is none of anyone's business. If she wants to remove all the books and take them up to her room, I am perfectly fine with that," he said.

The housekeeper gave him a look of disapproval. "Your father—the late Lord Glenbourne, may he rest in peace—said he didn't want the books removed or anyone using the library."

The earl smiled benevolently at the memory of his father at the end of his life. "Yes, and when he issued that dictum, he was in the beginning stages of dementia and could be unreasonable at times, but we did humor him. Now, I appreciate your loyalty to my father, but he has been gone now for a few years, and these are now my wishes."

"Very well, Lord Glenbourne," she replied tightly. And she gave him a slight bow and left the room.

Rachel wandered downstairs the following morning, still basking in the good time they'd had at dinner with Sammy and Trish. If only Thomas could ever feel for her the way she felt about him. He had played his part well. He had looked at her as if she were really beautiful, instead of someone you wouldn't cast a second glance at.

After breakfast, Rachel loaded her library books into her bag and headed off into the village. She managed to find a spot on the street in front of some terraced houses. It was a short walk to the library. Though the sidewalks were still wet from the previous night's rain, the clouds had lifted, and the sky was blue and the air cool.

As she stepped up onto the sidewalk, an elderly man exited his terraced house. He broke into a smile when he saw Rachel.

"You must be the new countess," he said. Rachel pegged him to be in his mid-eighties, with a shock of gray hair and watery blue eyes. His complexion was ruddy, and his hands were swollen. He wore a tweed cap and a heavy coat over gray pants and a black cardigan.

Rachel smiled. "I am."

The man doffed his cap and extended his hand. "Jer Lynch, Lady Glenbourne."

Rachel gently shook his hand. "Rachel Yates."

He gave her a grin and said, "It'll have to be Lady Glenbourne for me."

With a nod, she conceded defeat.

"I'm heading toward the newsagents myself," he said, nodding in the direction of the corner store.

"I'm going to the library," she replied.

"Do you like to read then?" he asked, looking at her with curiosity.

She nodded enthusiastically. "I do."

He seemed to take this under consideration. "The last countess, I don't think, was much of a reader. But then, they never really lived here. And when she was here, I don't ever remember her coming into the village." He stopped and so did

Rachel. He eyed her. "But you seem to spend a lot of time in the village."

"I like it. It's pretty."

He nodded. "We were all delighted when the present earl took up permanent residence in the manor. Everyone in the village hoped it would go back to the way it used to be."

"How do you mean?" Rachel asked, intrigued.

"When the 10th Earl of Glenbourne was alive—that'd be Lord Glenbourne's grandfather—he was considered one of us. He was on very good terms with the villagers. Every Sunday up at the manor was like an open house during the afternoon. Anyone from the village could go up and talk to the earl or ask for his advice. That sort of thing."

"It sounds lovely," Rachel said honestly.

They had reached the newsagents, and the man stopped. He stared off into the distance as if lost in a memory. "There'd be afternoon tea served for the visitors. We hoped it would be like that with his grandson, but we don't see him at all. Too much like his parents."

This affected Rachel, but she said nothing.

Jer regarded her with a twinkle in his eye. "But you're here now, and maybe all is not lost."

"Maybe," she said softly, thinking there was still some time to get things done. To solve problems. After all, that was what she was best at.

"Well, I've got to get inside to get my paper and a ticket for the Euro Millions. It's a big jackpot coming up."

Rachel smiled. "Good luck, Jer. I'll see you around."

"You will," he said, and he ambled into the shop.

Rachel thought about what the old man had said as she walked to the library. She hadn't realized that there was such a disconnect between the manor and the village. She chewed her lip as she walked up the footpath to the village library. She noticed two trucks with the words "County Council" written on them. The area on one side of the library was sealed off with tape, and scaffolding had been placed against the building.

As she entered the library and placed her books on the desk, she noticed the place was in a commotion. At the opposite end of the room, she could see the ominous, dark stains of water along the wall. Plaster piled on the floor, and two canvases for the exhibit lay against the wall, the damage obvious.

The librarian approached her. Her face was full of lines and there was a grim set to her mouth.

"Marian, what happened?" Rachel enquired.

The librarian groaned. "Major leak last night with all the rain. We discovered it as soon as we came in this morning."

"It's just awful," Rachel sympathized.

The librarian nodded in agreement. "It is. And our exhibit is planned for the night after tomorrow, and now we're going to have to cancel it. They can't have the repairs done in time."

"Oh no, that's awful," Rachel said. "Can you postpone it?"

The other woman shook her head. "It would be too difficult. There are too many artists involved, and we wanted to include the transition-year students. We may just have to write the whole affair off as a loss."

"All because you don't have a venue?" Rachel asked in disbelief.

The librarian nodded. "I already called to see if we could use the community center, but they're closed this week due to painting and repairs. And there really isn't anywhere else where we can exhibit all these paintings. We have almost fifty, so we'd need a pretty big space."

Rachel bit her lip. "I think I might be able to help."

The librarian looked at her, raising her eyebrows.

"I'd like to offer the ballroom at the manor to you for the exhibition. It will be ready to go by Thursday night," Rachel said, her mind beginning to spin as she thought about all that needed to be done.

"Lady Glenbourne, that is very gracious, but we couldn't impose," Marian protested.

Rachel waved her protest away with her hand. "Of course you can, and I'd be only too delighted to help." She stood with one hand on her hip and the finger of her other hand on her chin. "Now, we need someone from this end to organize it. And of course, we'll need to transport all the artwork." She was thinking aloud, but this was what set the wheels in motion.

The librarian spoke up. "May I suggest someone?"

"Yes, please," Rachel replied.

"See those paintings over there? The ones that were destroyed by the water?" Marian asked. Rachel looked and nodded in acknowledgement.

"Those were done by Agneta Blaszkiewicz, a young Polish girl who is full of incredible talent. She was distraught this morning when she saw the damage and is feeling a bit discouraged."

Rachel put her hand up. "Say no more. Have her meet me at the manor at ten tomorrow morning. Do you have a piece of paper?"

She scribbled down the number for the landline at the manor and handed it back. "This is the number of the manor; you can always reach me there. I don't have an Irish mobile yet, and it would be too expensive to call my American cell."

The woman nodded. "Lady Glenbourne, I can't thank you enough for coming to our rescue."

"Not at all. I'm more than happy to help," Rachel said. "If you can think of anything else, just let me know."

"This will be plenty, I'm sure."

Once Rachel had selected three more books, she left to return to the manor, thinking about how she would tell Thomas that she had just volunteered his home for a public art exhibit. Surely, he would have no problem with that.

CHAPTER NINE

"**Y**OU DID WHAT?" THOMAS asked later that evening over dinner. His fork and knife hovered over his plate as he looked at his wife in disbelief.

"I offered the use of the ballroom for the exhibit," Rachel said hurriedly. With her own fork and knife, she pushed the food around on her plate, avoiding his eyes. "They were in a bind. The library needs repairs, and it would never have been ready in two days' time."

He could not believe that in two days, his home was going to be overrun with villagers. He speared a piece of meat. "Did it ever occur to you to ask me if it was okay?"

She regarded him oddly. Smirking, she replied, "How would that have looked? 'Let me check with my husband and see if I have his permission'?"

"You could have said nothing, come back here, and discussed it with me," he said.

"And what would your answer have been?" she asked.

"No," he said.

"Ha! As I thought," she said. "What is the problem, exactly?"

He looked at her, not comprehending that she didn't get it. "This is my home. Not a community center."

"And this is your village. And these are your people," Rachel pointed out, eyes widening and voice tight.

He sighed. "I am not responsible for them.""Oh, Thomas, really? Doesn't the village bear your family name and crest?" she asked.

"The connection between the manor and village ceased a long time ago," he said, not looking at her.

"Maybe it's time to reconnect with your past," she suggested.

Thomas had had no idea that his bride was loaded with tenacity. If he had known, he might have chosen a more suitable candidate.

She continued. "I saw a wonderful exhibit in town about the symbiotic relationship between the Earls of Glenbourne and the village. It can be that way again."

Thomas shook his head.

Rachel continued. "They needed help, and we were in a position to provide it."

He sipped from his water glass. A quick glance around told him there were no staff about. He leaned toward her and lowered his voice. "I appreciate that you are a problem solver by nature, but remember, you are not here long-term, so don't get people's hopes and expectations up."

Tight-lipped, Rachel stood up and threw her napkin on the table.

"Rachel, please," he said. The last thing he wanted to do was fight with her. But he had to make her see that things were done differently here. And she was only there in a temporary capacity. Was she going to institute these changes and then just fly off back to America, leaving him to carry it forward?

As she turned, the door burst open, and Sammy Bolton-Wright burst through, looking distraught. Thomas immediately stood up and went to his friend, wondering what was the cause of his distress. Rachel was at his side.

Sammy turned toward Rachel. "What did you say to her?"

Rachel frowned, confused. "Who?"

"Trish," he wailed. He turned to Thomas. "She broke up with me today."

Thomas watched as Rachel paled, and he pressed his lips together in a grim line, wondering what indeed his new wife had said to Sammy's girlfriend.

"Did she say why?" Thomas asked.

Sammy shook his head. "No, she just said that she'd decided to take Rachel's advice and that it was over."

Thomas and Sammy leveled their gazes at Rachel.

Rachel reflexively took a step back.

"Rachel, what could you have said to a woman you met only once that caused her to break up her long-term relationship?" Thomas demanded.

"Well, um, let me see," Rachel said, thinking and stalling. "We were in the ladies' room—"

Sammy interrupted and turned to Thomas. "Do you see why they go off in pairs to the restroom? They're plotting our unhappiness!"

If the situation hadn't been so critical, Thomas would have laughed. But he managed to refrain.

Rachel stood with one hand on her hip and the other hand on her forehead, trying to recall their conversation in the powder room. "She asked me how I managed to get Thomas to the altar so quickly, when she couldn't get you to commit for the last five years," Rachel explained.

"But your marriage is fake," Sammy protested.

Thomas ignored the obvious and prompted Rachel. "And?"

"She said she felt that you had grown too comfortable in your relationship," Rachel said to Sammy.

Thomas noted that she had kindness written all over her face. He had to admit that he agreed with Trish.

Rachel continued. "She said she felt like you were taking her for granted."

Sammy appeared crestfallen.

Thomas, with his arms crossed and one finger on his lip, said to Rachel, "And did you say anything to that?"

Rachel looked from Thomas to Sammy and back and drew in a deep breath. "I may have said something along the lines of needing to shake you up a bit."

Thomas closed his eyes and groaned. His friend let out a howl of pain.

"I am truly sorry, Sammy," Rachel said. "I never thought she'd take what I said as gospel and run with it the very next day."

"Well, run with it she did," Sammy said. "What am I going to do without my Trish?"

Thomas looked at Rachel, and with exasperation in his voice, said, "Stop trying to solve things. Stop trying to fix things."

Unflinching, Rachel stepped closer to him and said evenly, "You're asking me not to help people. It's like asking me not to breathe." She turned to Sammy. "Now, I am truly sorry for your troubles, Sammy, but it sounds to me like you did need shaking up. If you want her back to resume the status quo, then the harsh reality is that it isn't going to happen. Go home and examine your conscience and decide once and for all if you want Trish as your lifetime partner. Not a part-time partner until someone or something better comes along. If you're truly interested in getting Trish back, I will help you. But only if you truly want her back."

Both men stood there speechless as she turned abruptly and exited the room with a determined walk and her head held high.

Sammy looked to Thomas. "Where on earth did you find her?"

His voice was a combination of awe, admiration, respect, and a bit of terror. Very similar to what Thomas was feeling.

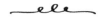

Rachel was fuming by the time she crawled into bed. Of course she felt terrible about Sammy, but he was his own worst enemy. What did men think? That women were just going to hang around wasting the best years of their lives waiting for a man to commit? Trish had done the right thing. Sammy was shaken up. And if after a good long think he decided he didn't want to make a commitment to her, then it was only fair to let her go and let her get on with her life.

But what had really made Rachel angry was Thomas's re-action to her offering the ballroom for the art exhibit. Why wouldn't he want to help his own people out? Why wouldn't you want to help people out in general? If she saw a need, she did something about it. Apathy toward others was one of her pet peeves.

She unwrapped a piece of caramel and popped it into her mouth. She chewed it thoughtfully, thinking about things. She heard the connecting door to the earl's room opening.

Quickly, she turned off the bedside light, slipped down into the bed, and pulled the covers up around her shoulders.

Thomas entered the darkened room and moved toward his spot on the chaise.

"No sense in pretending you're asleep, Rachel," he whispered. "I can hear you chewing, and I can smell candy."

She remained quiet until she heard him settle on the chaise. Suddenly, she felt tired.

"Are you angry?" he asked.

"Not angry," she said wearily. "Just a bit disappointed."

In the darkness, he sighed. "Things are done differently here. That's all."

It was her turn to sigh. "Maybe now. But it wasn't so long ago when it was different."

"What do you mean?" he asked.

"I was talking to one of the villagers today," she said. "A very nice man by the name of Jer. He had some lovely memories of your grandfather."

"My grandfather was a wonderful man," Thomas said.

Rachel continued. "He said the manor used to be open on Sunday afternoons for the villagers to come for a chat, and tea would be served."

Thomas didn't say anything, and for a moment Rachel wondered if he was angry at her for bringing it up, or maybe thinking back to a gentler time.

"Did your father not carry on the tradition?" she asked.

Thomas snorted. "My parents were nontraditional. They really had no interest in the manor or the village. They preferred Dublin, London, or Paris. Any place but here."

Rachel did not miss the bitterness in his voice. She bit her lip in the dark, thinking that it all sounded sad. She refrained from any criticism of his parents. "But yet, you yourself have made the manor your home."

"I've always loved it here."

"Don't you think it would be lovely to renew some of those traditions?" she asked gently.

The earl exhaled. "That was a long time ago, Rachel. People wouldn't be interested in that sort of thing now."

"Maybe not that sort of thing exactly, but I'd bet they'd be interested in some involvement of the present earl with the village."

"I am not my grandfather," he said from the chaise.

"Nobody is asking you to be your grandfather," she explained. "You're your own man. But by your own admission, your grandfather was pretty special. He was someone you were proud of. He set the example for you. His example—and it was a pretty damn good one—said, 'We are here for the people of our village. We are one with them.'"

Thomas said nothing.

"Again, no one is saying you have to be like him. But he gave you an example to live by. An honorable one. You can use that example as your template."

From her way of seeing things, she couldn't understand what was holding him back.

"My grandfather was a different person than my parents," he said.

"And?"

He remained silent.

"Twenty-five percent of you is made up of his genes," she said. "Sometimes all you need is one percent."

"What if it's not enough?"

"You'll never know unless you try," she said.

"But this room is just not used, Lady Glenbourne," Mrs. Brennan said from the midst of the grand ballroom.

Rachel refrained from rolling her eyes. Was it this woman's sole mission to butt heads with Rachel over everything? She was beginning to feel like the second Mrs. De Winter.

"I understand that, Mrs. Brennan, but we must help out where we can," Rachel said.

"And Lord Glenbourne is aware of all of this?"

Rachel bristled. "Of course he is. Now, if it's at all possible, this room will need to be cleaned and polished."

Mrs. Brennan was shaking her head, her lips pressed thin, before Rachel had even finished her sentence. "We are down two housemaids today," she said.

"Are they sick?" Rachel asked, concerned, hoping that nothing was going around.

The housekeeper shook her head. "No, child-care issues." She then added, "Supposedly."

Rachel tucked that away and would deal with it later. "Is there anyone here that can do it? That we can shift from another task?"

"It's only myself and Greta," Mrs. Brennan said.

Rachel sighed, aware that she was in a standoff with the woman. It was obvious that the housekeeper had no intention of redirecting staff or doing it herself.

Finally, Rachel said with determination, "I appreciate the situation, Mrs. Brennan. If you show me where the cleaning supplies are, I will tackle this room myself."

Mrs. Brennan's mouth fell open and stayed there. Her eyes widened and she said, "It would not do for Lady Glenbourne to be cleaning a room!"

"We'll need to put those things aside, as work needs to get done," Rachel said, not backing down.

"Excuse me, Lady Glenbourne," a voice called from the doorway.

Rachel and the housekeeper turned toward Mrs. Maher who, judging by the expression on her face, had witnessed the whole exchange.

"Yes, Mrs. Maher?" Rachel said with a smile, grateful for a friendly face.

"There is an Agneta Blaszkiewicz here to see you," the secretary answered.

"Perfect," Rachel said. "Would you mind showing her in here?"

"Not at all," said Mrs. Maher, disappearing out of the room.

Rachel turned to the housekeeper. "Can I ask for some tea and refreshments for our guest?"

Mrs. Brennan nodded. "Of course." Without looking at Rachel, she said, "I'll make sure the room is tidied up by the end of the day."

"Thank you, I appreciate that," Rachel said. "Can you please let Mrs. Shortt know that we will be entertaining tomorrow, and tea and refreshments will be needed?"

"Of course," Mrs. Brennan said, and without another word, she left the room.

The meeting with Agneta went well. Over tea and crustless sandwiches, they discussed what they hoped to accomplish with the exhibit. Rachel encouraged her not to despair over her lost paintings, that though it was a blow, she must go on. The girl was simply too talented to give up. After a while, as

Agneta got into organizing everything, her chatty demeanor began to shine through, and Rachel felt the spell of gloom over her damaged paintings lift from her.

The exhibit would open the following night at seven sharp and would run for two hours. New posters announcing the change in venue had been made up and tacked all over the village with the help of the transition-year students. They had rung the local village paper, as well, which would post the change in venue in its Thursday-morning edition. All in all, it was coming along nicely. In the meantime, Rachel had sourced some easels to display the artwork from local museums and colleges up and down their side of the country. Agneta's boyfriend, Martin, had a van, and he was en route to collect the items. With the help of some volunteers, all the paintings for the exhibit would be transported from the library to the manor first thing in the morning.

After Rachel saw Agneta to the door, she was intercepted by Mrs. Maher.

"Lady Glenbourne, Lord Glenbourne has asked to see you in his study. He said when you have a moment."

"Might as well see him now," Rachel said.

The two women walked side by side through the gallery.

"You seem to be adjusting to your new life," Mrs. Maher said with an approving smile.

Rachel returned the smile. "Just trying to help."

"It's very good of you to take it all on," the secretary said. "You strike me as someone who'll be hands-on at the manor. "They had arrived at the secretary's office.

"It's the kind of person I am," Rachel explained.

"Come inside for just a minute," Mrs. Maher requested. "I hope I don't offend you."

Rachel glanced at her with a puzzled expression. They stepped inside the secretary's office, and Rachel immediately noticed that a second desk had been installed, on the other side of the room.

The secretary explained. "I thought you might need an office or a base at the manor from which to conduct your own business. You can have your pick of the desks—"

Rachel was absolutely touched. The other woman's kindness left her momentarily speechless. "No, no, Mrs. Maher, it's perfect. I can't thank you enough."

Mrs. Maher looked pleased. "Now, of course, this could only be temporary if you would prefer your own office. And I'm only here three days a week anyway."

"If you don't mind, I'd prefer to share," Rachel said. She looked at the woman. "I'd like the company."

"Very good," Mrs. Maher said with a smile. "I'll get you a telephone for your desk, as well as some basic supplies."

Rachel reached out and touched her on the arm. "Again, Mrs. Maher, thank you so much."

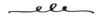

The earl watched as his friend, Sammy, lounged on the settee in front of the fire. He'd apparently made a decision: he wanted Trish back at all costs. And now that this decision had been made, Sammy's spirits had lifted a bit.

There was a knock, followed by Rachel entering the room. There was something about her that made Thomas take notice. Her eyes were bright, and her complexion had a rosy cast to it. When she smiled, her whole demeanor changed. She appeared content. And that got him thinking.

"You wished to see me, Thomas?"

He indicated toward Sammy, who jumped up from the settee. "You have company."

"Sammy! It's good to see you," Rachel said warmly, greeting him with a hug and a smile. Thomas found himself wondering what it would be like to be hugged by her. He pushed those thoughts, and others like it, to the outer recesses of his mind.

"Rachel," Sammy began in earnest. "I want her back. The truth is, I can't live without Trish. She's my reason for being."

Rachel laughed at his declaration in a good-humored way. "That's a start. At some point, you're going to need to tell her what you just told me."

His shoulders sagged. "Right now, she's not returning my calls."

"Give her some time."

"You said you'd help me get her back," he said to her.

"And I will," she said, putting her finger on her lip, thinking.

Thomas had to admit he couldn't wait to see what Rachel had up her sleeve. What was her grand plan to get his best friend back together with his girlfriend?

"Sit down, Sammy," Rachel said.

Sammy resumed his position on the settee and from his desk, Thomas watched as Rachel began to pace back and forth. With her familiar gesture of one hand on her hip and the index and thumb of the other hand against her lip, Rachel paced.

"All right, let's see what we've got. Trish feels like you're dragging your feet. She feels like you don't want to commit. And most of all, she feels like you've taken her for granted," Rachel said, laying the facts out before them.

Sammy winced.

"I've been a fool. Her leaving me has done me a favor. I realize now how much Trish means to me."

Thomas hoped Sammy wouldn't start crying again. His friend had become unhinged with the breakup.

Rachel spoke. "I think what's needed here is a grand gesture."

"A grand gesture?" Sammy repeated.

Thomas himself was intrigued.

"When it comes to romance, there is nothing a woman loves more than a grand gesture. It's something that says a man has been paying attention to what is most important to his woman." She had a faraway look in her eyes. Wistfully, she added, "It can be a game changer."

Sammy appeared mesmerized. "Okay, tell me what kind of grand gesture I need to make."

Rachel shook her head. "If I come up with your grand gesture for Trish, it won't work. You have to think of something yourself."

All sorts of thoughts were barreling around in Thomas's head. Grand gestures?

"Can you help me out?" Sammy asked, a pleading tone in his voice. "Give me some direction."

"Well, since she's already broken up with you, it will have to be an especially grand gesture," Rachel said. "Like, say she's always hinting at the two of you going somewhere romantic, and you agree in theory, but you never do anything about it. It's always the same old, same old."

Sammy winced and Thomas could see that his wife had already hit a nerve.

"Or maybe her family is extremely important to her but not to you," Rachel said, still pacing.

Thomas wondered if she spoke from personal experience.

"Maybe she likes public displays of affection, and you don't," Rachel continued.

"I don't actually, but she does go for all that stuff," Sammy said, making a face.

Rachel stopped in her tracks. "You'll have to get over that. Public displays of affection do not mean mauling your partner. It can be something simple like a light touch or handholding, so everyone knows you're together."

"I see what you mean, Rachel," Sammy said.

"Does this give you some idea of the direction you need to go?" she asked him.

It certainly gave Thomas a lot of ideas.

"Do you think you can manage?" she asked.

Sammy nodded, enthused. "Thank you for your help. I'll let you know how I get on." He stood up from the settee and said his goodbyes, leaving Thomas alone with Rachel. "Very good." She smiled. "Now, I need to get back to organizing this exhibit."

CHAPTER TEN

T HERE WAS A BUSTLE of activity in the hours preceding the art exhibit. Thomas remained in his office, trying to ignore the whirl of activity that consumed the manor. There was a steady stream of volunteers from the village, and a group of secondary students who walked back and forth from the front of the manor down the long gallery to the grand ballroom.

"I can't ever remember seeing the manor so busy," Mrs. Maher said, entering his study and laying a pile of paperwork on his desk.

"Me neither," Thomas said. At least, not since his grandfather had been alive. He wasn't sure yet how he felt about it. On one hand, he resented the intrusion, wary of people invading his privacy. On the other hand, it reminded him of a happy time.

"There's a certain buzz in the air," Mrs. Maher was saying. "Like it's almost Christmas. Lady Glenbourne is certainly a force to be reckoned with."

"She certainly is," he agreed. It seemed to him as though Rachel had been living at the manor her whole life. The role of Lady Glenbourne came naturally to her, which he hadn't expected. She still suffered bouts of homesickness; he knew that only too well by the red eyes he saw at times, but she didn't lie around and wallow. She threw herself into things. He'd begun to see her in a different light.

He hoped she didn't expect him to partake of the evening's activities. He was torn. He had no desire to mingle, but he felt obligated as the Earl of Glenbourne to play host. But certainly, she couldn't be expecting that? He'd remain in his study, working on the merger. And if the spirit moved him, he might pop in and say a quick hello.

Thomas knew the event was starting at seven. From the windows in his study, he could see the sweep of headlights as cars pulled in and parked at the front of the manor. That was followed by the continuous noise of car doors slamming. Sighing, he put down his pen. He couldn't concentrate. He stepped out into the main hall, where the noise grew louder. He was surprised at the number of people traipsing to the grand ballroom.

He was just about to return to his study when he saw Rachel coming toward him, wearing her coat and hat.

"Are you going somewhere?" he asked.

"Ugh, I've got to go into the village. There must have been a mix-up in communication. Mrs. Shortt never got the message that I was going to need baked goods for tonight."

Thomas thought she looked tired. He knew she'd put a lot of effort into this exhibit in a short amount of time. And the last thing she'd want was to look like a fool.

"Can I ask a favor?" she asked, her eyes pleading.

Thomas was wary. Her favors wouldn't be simple, he was sure. It might involve single-handedly building an irrigation system in a third-world country, or donating part of the estate for a wildlife preserve.

She laughed. "Thomas, don't look at me like that. You'd think I was going to ask you for a kidney!"

"Okay, what?" he asked, still cautious.

Rachel nodded in the direction of the grand ballroom. "Can you just play host for ten minutes until I return?"

"I'd rather give you my kidney," he replied.

She tilted her head and smiled. "Just til I return?"

He sighed. "All right. Just this once."

"Of course," she said. She leaned in and placed a kiss on his cheek, startling him. "Thank you so much."

He drew in a deep breath and headed to the ballroom, reminding himself that this was a one-off. He could play gracious host for a few minutes. Besides, in a few months, all would go back to normal. And deep down inside of him, that's what he was really afraid of.

Later that evening after the exhibit had ended, Rachel and Thomas kicked back in the study with a glass of wine.

"It feels so good to sit down and get off my feet," Rachel said, kicking off her heels. Max curled up at her feet.

Thomas eyed her shoes. "I don't know how you stand in those things, let alone run back and forth between the rooms."

Rachel smiled. "Yes, but they look good."

"They do indeed," he agreed.

Rachel sank back among the pillows, holding her glass of wine. For the first time since arriving at the manor, she felt content.

The evening had been a huge success. The grand ballroom had been packed with not only villagers but some members of the press and people from other localities. The artists had stood next to their work and greeted people. Marian the librarian was there, running back and forth and making sure everything and everyone was in place. Even the vicar had put in an appearance, offering his support.

After she'd returned from town with loads of baked goods, she'd handed them off to the secondary students, who assembled them on silver trays with paper doilies. There were coffee and tea urns set up in the gallery.

Upon her return, she'd been pleased to see Thomas chatting to some of the villagers. If he would only give it a chance, she thought.

When Jer Lynch ambled in, Rachel introduced him to her husband, and soon the two of them were reminiscing about Thomas's grandfather. And although Rachel suspected some only came to get a peek inside the manor, all of the artwork had been sold. Even Agneta had managed to showcase two other pieces from her portfolio.

"Congratulations, Rachel," Thomas said, clinking his glass to hers.

"Thank you for everything," she said. She saw him in a new light and felt there was hope for him.

After her return, he'd remained in the ballroom for another half hour, talking to artists, students, and villagers. He was a natural in his role and just hadn't known it. She'd caught snippets of his conversations and was surprised at how charming he'd been. Some of the older women of the village appeared completely smitten with him. It was easy to see why: the classical looks, the strong jaw, those amazing blue eyes, and his impeccable manners.

They'd met up, and he'd put his hand on the small of her back, leaned into her, and whispered that she had done a wonderful job. The compliment, combined with the touch, had been the only wobble of the evening. Rachel's legs had gone to jelly with the feel of his hand on her back and his warm breath against her neck. For a moment, she'd forgotten about her role, and thoughts about kissing him flooded her mind. This surprised her, and she chalked it up to the excitement of the evening.

They sat back, sipping their wine, saying nothing, both exhausted and staring at the orange flames of the fire shooting up at the chimney. Even the dog was tired from the day's events and had fallen asleep on Rachel's foot.

"Well, I'm going to head up to bed," the earl said, rising from the settee and breaking the spell. Rachel looked up at him, something forming in her mind that she wasn't quite ready to acknowledge. "I've got to be in Dublin tomorrow."

"I'll stay on a bit if you don't mind," she said, watching him.

"Not at all," he said. "Again, my heartfelt congratulations on your success."

"Thank you. It's your success as well as mine," she said.

"Hardly," he said. "Goodnight, Rachel."

The morning after the exhibit, Thomas left for Dublin and Mrs. Maher was off for the day.

Rachel found herself in the kitchen with Mrs. Brennan and Mrs. Shortt. Although she suspected Mrs. Brennan had con-

veniently forgot to inform the cook about the need for refreshments, she could not go around making accusations. She
had to be careful with the staff. Though she was technically in
charge, she'd be back in the US before they got used to her and
her ways.

Mrs. Shortt cast a sideways glance at the housekeeper. Her
face reddened, and she said, "Lady Glenbourne, I am so sorry
for the confusion. I misunderstood. I did not get the message
that refreshments were needed for the exhibit."

Both Rachel and the cook looked to the housekeeper, who
appeared rattled. "I'm so sorry, Lady Glenbourne. I forgot.
With trying to get the grand ballroom ready, it slipped my
mind."

Rachel decided it wasn't a hill worth dying on. "Never mind.
Perhaps in the future, you should carry a notebook to write
things down, so you can remember then," Rachel said gently.

Mrs. Brennan bristled and said tightly, "I assure you, there
is nothing wrong with my memory. If I wasn't trying to plug
holes in staffing—"

"What's going on with the staff?" Rachel queried.

"The same problems. They have children who are sick, or
they don't have a childminder in the first place," Mrs. Brennan
explained.

"Well, I can certainly understand a mother wanting to be
with her sick child," Rachel said.

"I can too, but maybe in the future, the manor should hire
staff without children," Mrs. Brennan suggested.

Rachel paled. "That would be discrimination, Mrs. Brennan."

The housekeeper's face went the color of puce, and even the
cook looked alarmed.

Before the housekeeper could blow, Rachel said, "Have the staff who have been absent come to my office at eleven. I'd also like to see any staff who have children school age or younger."

"Very well then, Lady Glenbourne," Mrs. Brennan said tightly. "And where is your office?"

"I'm sharing an office with Mrs. Maher."

As Rachel followed her out, Mrs. Shortt hurried after her.

"Lady Glenbourne, may I have a word with you?"

"Of course," Rachel said.

The cook lowered her voice. "It's about Margaret . . . um, I mean, Mrs. Brennan."

"Yes?" Rachel asked, curious.

Mrs. Shortt fingered her apron nervously. "Mrs. Brennan most likely did forget."

"All right then," Rachel said, not yet convinced.

"She's very stressed out," the cook said. "And she'll tear the strips off of me when she finds out I told you."

"What is she stressed about?" Rachel asked.

"It's her sister, Breda. She's having a mastectomy next week in England, and Mrs. Brennan is so upset she can hardly think straight. Since her husband died over twenty years ago, Mrs. Brennan takes her holidays every year with her sister in Brighton." The cook paused and added, "They're very close. It's the only family Mrs. Brennan has."

"Why doesn't she go over to England and stay with her?" Rachel asked.

Mrs. Shortt snorted. "Mrs. Brennan take a day off? She takes her two weeks' holidays every August, and that's it. She's been here almost thirty years, and she's never missed a day."

"That's admirable," Rachel said truthfully. She thought for a moment and said to the cook, "Thank you for letting me know. I'll take care of this."

After Rachel had an hour-long meeting with the staff, which proved to be very productive, she summoned the housekeeper to the office she shared with Mrs. Maher.

Mrs. Brennan appeared in the doorway. "You wished to see me, Lady Glenbourne?"

"Come in, Mrs. Brennan," Rachel said with a wave of her hand. "And please, sit down."

The housekeeper stood in front of Rachel's desk and said, "I'd prefer to stand, Lady Glenbourne."

Tapping her pen on the desk, Rachel looked at her and said softly, "And I would prefer you to sit down."

A moment passed before the other woman finally relented and sat down. Rachel let go of the breath she'd been holding.

Rachel stood up and closed the door. "I'd like to talk to you privately."

She did not miss the look of alarm on the housekeeper's face.

"Lady Glenbourne, I truly did forget about the refreshments for the exhibition," she said hurriedly. "It won't happen again, I assure you."

Rachel nodded, sitting back down in her chair. "I know. But that's not why I want to talk to you."

Mrs. Brennan stiffened.

"Mrs. Brennan, it has come to my attention that you have some important issues going on in your personal life," Rachel said, aware that she had to tread very carefully with the other woman.

"And where did you hear this?" the housekeeper demanded.

"It doesn't matter," Rachel said. "What matters is you have a sick sister."

Mrs. Brennan's demeanor crumbled. Her mouth opened, but no words came out.

"Why didn't you come to me and ask me for some time off to go to your sister?" Rachel asked.

"Because I don't take time off from work," she replied.

Rachel decided to try a different tack. "Would you like to be with your sister when she has her surgery?"

Finally, Mrs. Brennan relented and said, "I would."

"When is her surgery?" Rachel asked.

"Next week."

"All right," Rachel said. "I think you should take the week off and go be with your sister."

Mrs. Brennan opened her mouth to protest, but Rachel cut her off. "You will be paid for the full week."

"It's not the pay, Lady Glenbourne," the housekeeper said.

Rachel frowned. "Is there something else?"

The housekeeper sighed, squared her shoulders, and looked straight at Rachel.

"I'm afraid I'd be out of a job when I came back."

"Why would you be out of a job?" Rachel asked.

"Well, I'd be replaced."

"Why?" Rachel asked, clearly perplexed.

Mrs. Brennan could only shrug.

Rachel regarded the other woman for a moment and asked, "In the thirty years you've worked at the manor, has anyone ever thanked you for your service? Told you you were doing a great job?"

Mrs. Brennan's shoulders sagged. "I'm not here for the thanks."

"I know."

Both women stared at each other, and finally Rachel said, "Well, I'm going to tell you. You're an excellent housekeeper. The place would fall apart if you weren't here."

The housekeeper reddened and looked away. "Thank you, Lady Glenbourne. I appreciate that."

"But," Rachel continued, "family is the most important thing. As much as you love your job, I think you'd prefer to be at your sister's side."

Mrs. Brennan's chin quivered. "I would."

"All right then," Rachel said, feeling like they were getting somewhere. "Take a week off. Longer, if you need to or want to. Your job will be here when you get back, I assure you."

"Thank you, Lady Glenbourne. I don't know what to say."

"You don't need to say anything. But please go, and don't worry about the manor," Rachel advised.

"I can't help it," Mrs. Brennan said, standing up from her chair.

"Have one of the housemaids step up and fill in while you're gone," Rachel instructed.

Mrs. Brennan nodded. "I will."

Before she left, she looked at Rachel and said, "Thank you again for your kindness, Lady Glenbourne."

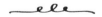

Once the success of the exhibit died down and the earl returned from Dublin, everything went back to normal. Getting more adventurous, Thomas cooked up bangers and mash one evening for Rachel.

Rachel's eyes widened when he set the plate down in front of her.

"It's a traditional Irish dish, bangers and mash," he said, nodding toward the mashed potatoes, pork sausage, and onion gravy. He'd made a side dish of mushy peas with mint.

As rain hit the dining-room windows, Rachel said, "Perfect comfort food for a night like tonight."

Thomas was secretly pleased. What surprised him was that he enjoyed cooking. More than that, he liked cooking for her. She was so appreciative, and no matter what he served, she was enthused. He found himself googling recipes to cook. Granted, he was no Nigella Lawson, but he had graduated from grilled cheese and packet soup.

"This is delicious," Rachel said, forking food into her mouth.

It continued to rain.

"Have you heard from Sammy?" Rachel asked.

Thomas shook his head. "No news is good news."

"I suppose," Rachel said. She frowned. "I hope it all works out."

Without thinking, Thomas reached over and placed his hand over hers. She looked up at him, surprised. "The fact that we haven't heard from him is a good thing," he said. He pulled his hand away, not looking at her.

After a few moments of silence, Rachel announced with a laugh, "My youngest niece is going to be a turkey in the Thanksgiving play at her school."

"You miss your family, don't you?" he asked.

She nodded. "I do. And I'd love to see her perform. She's a natural ham."

"Would you like to go over?" he asked, wanting her to be happy.

She shook her head. "No, no. My sister-in-law has promised to videotape it for me and send it on."

"Are you still homesick?" he asked.

"Not as much," she said. "I text them every day, but it's not the same.""No, of course," he said, his voice drifting off. As much as he was growing fond of her, it would never work. It could never work. He could never ask her to leave the family she loved so much.

The following morning, Thomas sat at his executive desk, writing the legal document for the merger. Distracted by a noise outside his office, he paused and tilted his head, trying to place it. It didn't sound like Max, and looking around, he realized he hadn't a clue as to where Max was. Probably with Rachel. He knew Max to be a loyal dog but with Rachel, the loyalty had graduated to singular devotion. He shook his head in disappointment. There it was again: a high-pitched squeal followed by laughter. Laying his pen down on the desk, he pushed his chair back and stood up. Determined to investigate, he exited the study, and as he did, a heavy-diapered toddler went flying by along the gallery, chased by one of the housemaids. His mouth fell open.

The maid stopped running, pulling herself upright and appearing sheepish. "Lord Glenbourne, excuse me," she said.

"What was that that just went by?" Thomas asked.

The maid, whose name was Laura, looked down the corridor, keeping an eye on the child, and then looked quickly back at Thomas. "That's my little boy, Davey."

"And?" he asked, searching for enlightenment but getting no satisfaction.

"And?" Laura asked, clearly confused.

Thomas sighed. "What is he doing here?"

The maid stammered, her face reddening. "He's in the day-care."

Thomas blinked, not once, not twice, but three times. "Day-care? There's a daycare in the manor?"

"Yes," the maid said, taking a step back. "Lady Glenbourne opened up a daycare for staff the other day. On a temporary basis."

"I see," Thomas said. There were a lot of things he could have said, all of which would have disparaged Rachel, but he came from an upbringing where one did not air one's dirty laundry in public, especially to staff. Besides, they were supposed to be madly in love. "It must have slipped my mind."

"Yes, Lord Glenbourne," she said, her eyes nervously darting down the gallery.

"Can you tell me where I might find Mrs. Brennan?" he asked.

"Mrs. Brennan isn't here."

"She isn't?"

The housemaid shook her head, glancing down the corridor to keep her eye on the little boy. "No, Lady Glenbourne gave her a week of compassionate leave to be with her sister. I'm filling Mrs. Brennan's shoes if you need anything."

He shook his head. "You'd better go round up Davey," he said. *Before he gets lost in the manor and we have to call in a search-and-rescue team.*

The maid took off running down the gallery.

Thomas marched to the office shared by his wife and Mrs. Maher. Rachel was behind her desk, looking at her computer screen and talking on the phone. She gave him a smile and a wave. It was hard to be mad at her for anything when she was so *nice*. But to start a daycare in the manor without consulting him really was going too far.

Mrs. Maher peered at them over the tops of her glasses. She didn't miss much.

Rachel covered the mouthpiece of the handset with her hand. "Do you need me, Thomas?"

"I know you're busy," he said, then he stopped. What was she doing on the phone, and who was she talking to? Was she planning on turning the no-longer-used west wing into a retirement home? He'd have to keep a closer eye on her. With a nod of his head over his shoulder, he asked, "May I have a word?"

"Of course." She smiled. "I'll be there in five minutes."

He hadn't been back to his study for long when she knocked on the door and entered. She wore a black pencil skirt with a feminine blouse. He forced himself to pay attention and not to be distracted by how pretty she looked.

"How can I help?" she asked.

He laughed. She was dangerous. That was a leading question with her, he'd found out after a few short weeks. That's what Rachel Parker lived for: to help.

He scratched his forehead. "Actually, I was hoping you could enlighten me about a couple of things."

With a reassuring smile, she said, "I'll try my best."

If things were different, if he had married her because he loved her, she would have been the ideal wife. More like a partner. But he hadn't married for love. He'd married out of necessity. Because he'd needed to preserve his estate and heritage. Another thing he was desperate to preserve was the status quo.

"Did you give Mrs. Brennan a week off?" he asked.

"I did," she said. "Her sister is having surgery, and she wanted to be with her."

"I did not know she even had a sister," he admitted, embarrassed.

"It was an on-the-spot decision," Rachel explained. "She never takes time off."

He could see she was not going to back down. He'd let this one slide. He wasn't a total ogre in regard to his staff. If they needed time off for personal reasons, then they needed time off. He couldn't ever remember Mrs. Brennan missing a day.

"There was a second thing?" Rachel asked.

"Earlier, a toddler ran by, last seen heading in the direction of the long gallery," he said, noting her reaction. Her smile slowly disappeared, and her lips parted slightly, which he found distracting.

"I can explain, Thomas," she began.

He leaned forward at his desk. "Please do."

"I saw a need," she said.

"I'm sure you did," he said, not smiling.

"There was a problem with staffing," she explained. "There was a high rate of absenteeism among the staff due to children's illnesses and babysitting problems."

"And you thought opening a daycare on-site was the solution," he said tightly. He didn't know what he was annoyed with more: the fact that she hadn't even run it by him or the fact that she was so compelled to *fix* everything.

"Possibly," she conceded. "I had a meeting with the staff who have children—"

Thomas looked sharply at her. "You had a meeting with manor staff, did you? Kind of presumptuous?"

Rachel swallowed. "I did. Now before you panic—"

"Before I panic? Did it not ever occur to you that you might want to run the idea by me before you instituted it?" he said, his voice rising slightly.

"It did, but I decided against it," she admitted.

He was stunned. The woman had no shame. "You decided against it? You're a guest in my home, and you've made decisions regarding my staff without consulting me?" This infuriated him.

She had the decency to look embarrassed.

"Please, Ms. Parker, do go on as to your reasoning for why I shouldn't be told," he directed. She flinched at the use of her maiden name. But he didn't care that he didn't feel very gallant at the moment.

She lowered her voice so much that he had to strain to hear her. "If I had come to you with a way to make things better here for your staff and ultimately you, you would have said no. If I'd said we could hire a villager with the right qualifications to run the daycare for the staff, that it would give someone a job and allow staff to see their children throughout the day, you would have said no."

"Not necessarily," he shot back.

She tilted her head to one side and said, "Thomas, really? You would have shot my idea down and we both know it."

He hated that she was right. He looked at her. "So you went behind my back instead? You thought that was the way to get it by me?"

She was shaking her head. "No. I told the staff that it would be a thirty-day pilot program to see how it worked. And at the end of the thirty days, the final decision would be up to you." She paused, eyed him, and said, "And no one else." "Well, that's big of you," he said. "And what if it's successful? Then I'm the bad guy for dismantling it?" He knew he sounded petulant, but he couldn't help it.

"If it's successful, why would you want to dismantle it? If your staff are happy, you'll get loyalty and better service, and both you and the manor would benefit from that," she cried.

He turned his back on her, choosing instead to cast his gaze out the window, at the fabulous grounds of his beloved manor.

He heard her step closer behind him. "Thomas, why do you hate change so much? What are you afraid of?"

Turning abruptly to face her, he was caught off-guard by the concern on her face. Ignoring her question, he said, "Close it down today, Rachel. I don't care what you tell them but close it down. You can blame it on me for all I care."

There was a muscle tic at the corner of her mouth. Her lips were pressed into a tight line. When she didn't respond, he added, "In the future, please do not make any decisions regarding my home or my staff without consulting me first."

"As you wish, my lord," she said quietly, and turned and left the room.

CHAPTER ELEVEN

M ID-NOVEMBER, RACHEL FOUND HERSELF with the run of the manor one Sunday afternoon. Thomas had gone up to Dublin on Thursday and was working through the weekend. He'd told her he wouldn't be back until late Sunday night. Things had been slightly frosty between them as of late. She was glad for the breather. She had closed down the daycare immediately, as he had requested, and took the disappointment of the staff to heart. She hated that he was right. It was his home, and she'd had no right to charge in and take over. She kept a low profile and any further staffing or manor issues she deferred to the earl. But it didn't mean she couldn't get involved with the village.

Most of the staff had the day off. She walked to the village in the morning for the Sunday papers, a couple of bags of candy, and a box of treats for Max. In the afternoon, she walked the grounds of the manor with the dog at her side. She thought of going back into the village to grab some dinner but immediately dismissed the idea. Her eating dinner alone in the village might not bode well for Thomas.

She spoke to Amy on the phone, learning that ground had been broken on the site for their new house. Her best friend sounded so much more relaxed. She rang her parents and her brothers and spoke to everyone. Finally, when she'd finished all her phone calls, she wandered down to the kitchen in search of some dinner.

The kitchen was empty, but there was a note from Mrs. Shortt saying there was a shepherd's pie in the fridge that only needed to be heated.

Removing the dish from the fridge, Rachel said, "Thank you, Mrs. Shortt."

Once the oven was preheated, she slid the dish in on a rack. She looked over at the dog. "It's just you and me for dinner, Max. I hope you like shepherd's pie."

The dog glanced at her, tongue hanging out and tail wagging.

Afterward, full, she settled into one of the big easy chairs in the drawing room and waited for *Dancing with the Stars,* the newfound guilty pleasure she indulged in on Sunday evenings.

She sat sideways in the wing chair, her legs over the arm, playing with her hair as she watched the couples dancing. It looked like so much fun. To be held in someone's arms!

Her mother came to mind, and her throat tightened. She missed her. Her mother had watched the American version of this show for years. Many times, she had asked Rachel to watch it with her, but Rachel had always declined, preferring to read. Rachel promised herself that when she returned home, she would make a point of watching it with her mother. They would have snacks and drinks and pass comments on the couples, their costumes, and their dance routines.

Deciding she just didn't want to be depressed about how much she missed her family, Rachel bounced out of her chair.

Watching the TV, she started whirling around the limited space of the drawing room, her arms in the air, dancing with an imaginary partner.

She closed her eyes and continued to spin, humming to the music. But she managed to spin right into the arms of the earl.

"Oh!" she said, eyes opening and face reddening. He had caught hold of her and did not immediately let go. His arms held her and his fingers pressed gently into the flesh above her elbows. For a moment, their eyes locked, and Rachel could feel the heat rising within her as she got lost in those azure-blue eyes of his. If she continued to look into his eyes, she feared she would end up scorched. Reluctantly, she stepped back, but she tripped over the corner of the coffee table and lost her balance. The earl reached out and grabbed her, his hand on her lower back, pulling her back up to a standing position.

"Thank you," she whispered.

"My pleasure," he said. The way he said it, with his delicious accent, left her flustered.

She stepped back and averted her eyes. "You're back early." She hoped she didn't sound accusatory.

"We finished early, and I was anxious to get home," he explained, not taking his eyes off of her.

"Oh."

"Do you like to dance?" he asked, nodding toward the television.

"I do, but I'm not very good at it," she admitted. She folded her arms across her chest, suddenly feeling very foolish.

"How do you know?" he asked.

"Just a feeling I get about myself." She laughed.

He tapped his fingers on the back of the club chair opposite her. "Don't you ever get bored?"

"With what?" she asked.

"With sitting around here every night."

"Sometimes," she replied.

"Would you like to go into the village to the pub for a drink?"

"I don't think so; I wouldn't feel comfortable going into a pub by myself," she said.

He laughed. "No, I meant with me." He looked at her intently.

"Oh. All right," she said. She picked up the throw that had fallen on the floor, folded it, and set it down on the chair. "I suppose it might be nice to get out for a bit."

"I think so," he agreed. "We don't want people thinking I've locked you up in the tower or something."

She winced. Of course. It was all about appearances. Why on earth would she ever think that he was asking *her* out? *You foolish girl*.

"I'll just get my coat and purse," she said.

She ran up the staircase to her room, brushed her teeth and her hair, and fixed her headband in place. After quickly changing her clothes and freshening up her makeup, she left the room with her coat and purse slung over her arm.

The earl stood in the main hall and looked up at her as she made her way down the staircase.

"I'm ready," she said. She set her purse down on the bottom step of the grand staircase and began to put her coat on, but the earl took it from her and held it for her. "Thank you," she said, a little breathless from running up and down all the stairs.

On the short drive over to the village, Thomas enquired how she'd been the past few days, and she filled him in on what was going on at the manor.

"We'll try the hotel," the earl said. "They have music on Sunday nights."

"That's fine," she said. *Boy, I am boring, I have absolutely nothing to add to the conversation.*

"Will I drop you off at the door?" he asked as he pulled up to the hotel.

"Of course not," she said, "I'm perfectly capable of walking from the parking lot."

"I didn't mean to offend; I was just trying to be—"

"Chivalrous? Gallant?" she asked, filling in the blanks.

He rewarded her with a smile, and she tried not to melt. "Maybe just polite."

We always seem to get off on the wrong foot. There was a lot of miscommunication and each thinking the other meant something else. It was a good thing they were only going to be together for a short time.

Thomas parked the car, and the two of them walked around to the front. "Hotel" was a loose description. It was a two-story building done up in various shades of cream with dark-green shutters and window boxes, which were now empty.

They walked side by side up the main steps into the hotel lobby, furnished with upholstered chairs scattered over a floral carpet. Thomas led her to the back of the hotel, where a long bar spanned the far wall next to an open area with a wood floor. Upholstered booths and high tables with stools ran the length of the opposite wall. The whole thing was done up tastefully in navy, lime green, and gray. Rachel looked down at the floor; there seemed to be a lot of wasted space. Some of the tables were empty, and there were a few people lined up at the bar, served by bartenders in white shirts with green aprons and black bow ties.

Interest was raised as soon as they walked through the door, and Rachel felt all eyes on them. The earl moved a bit closer to her and put his arm protectively around her waist. No matter how much she enjoyed him touching her, Rachel knew it was only for public consumption.

"Will we sit in a booth? It's a little more private," Thomas said.

He stood so close to her that she could smell his aftershave, and it was a heady experience. His dark hair curled at his collar, and she wanted to reach out and run her fingers through it. *Pull yourself together, Rachel,* she told herself.

"That's fine," she said, aware of eyes on her.

The earl stepped up to the bar, and the bartender nodded at him.

"Rachel, what will you have to drink?" he asked.

For a moment, she almost pulled out her wallet, but knew that image would be disastrous.

"A white wine, please," she said, standing next to him at the bar. She was dressed in a print dress that hugged her curves and showcased her legs. Looking around, she felt a bit out of place.

They carried their drinks to one of the last available booths and slid in on opposite sides of the bench until they met in the middle. Thomas inched closer to Rachel until his thigh brushed up against hers. In response, her knees went weak.

"Sorry," he said. He gave her an impish grin. "All eyes are on us, and I don't want to give them anything to talk about."

"Of course not," she said, trying to distract herself from thinking about sitting so close to someone she was crushing on. She felt like a hormonal teenager. For her, he ticked all the boxes. Her thoughts and feelings made her realize how seriously her life in the US had been in a rut. But just because he had movie-star good looks didn't mean he was worthy of her attention. After all, for Rachel, it was all about how people treated other people. When she returned home, she would certainly have a rethink of things. Like her love life. Or lack of one.

In the corner, a musician went about setting up his equipment. She was glad to see it, as she found it strange being in a bar and there being no music. For now, the amiable chatter of the patrons filled the void.

She realized the earl was speaking to her, and she turned her head toward him and blinked. "I'm sorry?"

He smiled. "How do you like living in Ireland?"

She nodded enthusiastically. "I love it. But I miss my family."

"Of course you do," he said.

She picked up her glass and sipped her wine. "One of my ancestors or another came from Ireland."

Thomas laughed. "I hear there are a lot of Americans with some form of Irish ancestry. Do you like to travel?"

"I never did," she said. "But since I've come over to Ireland, I'm now anxious to check out the rest of the world."

"Did your family drag you along on trips, growing up?" he asked.

"Well, my parents have a summer cottage out at the lake, so we spent a lot of time there. It was so nice that I really never wanted to go anywhere else," she explained.

He regarded her thoughtfully.

"Do you travel?" she asked.

"I like to, but I'm too busy with work to do much of it. I do go away on holiday every year," he said.

"Where do you go?" she asked.

"I usually go to the continent," he said, bringing his pint glass up to his lips. "France, Italy, Germany. You'd love it there; there's lots of history. Everything is so old."

"I probably would," she murmured in agreement. If anything, coming to Ireland had opened her eyes to all that lay out there to be discovered. All that history just waiting to be explored.

The music started, and the man behind the mic had a great voice. He also had a penchant for singing covers of American musicians: Elvis Presley, Neil Diamond, Johnny Cash, to name a few. It made Rachel think of home. A lump formed in her throat. Thomas stood up to get a second round of drinks, and she was relieved to be alone for a few moments. It was nerve-wracking sitting so close to someone she felt attracted to.

When he returned, he handed her her wine glass and settled back into the spot he had just vacated.

The musician shifted his focus toward Irish songs, and although Rachel did not recognize any of them, she soon found herself tapping her foot under the table to the rhythm.

A few couples stood up and began to dance in the middle of the floor. Now it made sense to Rachel why there was so much floor space. It was for dancing. She watched intently as the couples, mostly older ones, swirled expertly around the dance floor. There was a wonderful energy, and each couple was perfectly in sync with each other from years of dancing together.

"Would you like to dance?" Thomas asked her.

Rachel looked alarmed. Appearing in public for the gossip-mongers was one thing, but dancing in public? That was a whole different type of beast. "Oh no, I couldn't," she protested.

"Why not?" he asked.

"Because I don't know how to dance like that," she said.

"You told me you enjoy dancing," he said.

"I do," she said.

"Are you really so terrible at it?" he asked.

She laughed. "I'm passable, but *Dancing with the Stars* has nothing to worry about."

He let out a bark of laughter, which she responded to with a grin. A few heads turned in their direction to see what the earl had found so funny.

"Look, I know these steps and I think we should dance," he said. "They're basic Irish waltz steps."

She narrowed her eyes at him.

"Honestly, I have no hidden agenda," he assured her. "It's just that if you enjoy something, why not do more of it? Rather than sitting home watching *Dancing with the Stars*, why don't you go out dancing?"

It reminded her of her promise to herself to try new things. She almost resented him for it. Almost. But not quite.

He slid out of the booth, held out his hand, and said, "Come on Rachel, dance with me."

When he put it like that, she had no reason not to oblige him. She stood up and laid her hand in his. Her heart rate picked up and she wished he could touch her without her body having an automatic response. As inconvenient and awkward as it was, she'd be lying if she said she didn't enjoy it.

When they reached the dance floor, he pulled her closer to him in a tight embrace, and her heart pounded in response. Close to him, their bodies pressed together, every sense within her heightened and every nerve ending felt as if it was on fire. It reminded her of when she was younger—eighteen, twenty—when she'd been just waiting for something to happen.

"Just relax and follow my lead," he whispered, his breath warm on her ear.

Looking around the dance floor and seeing eyes on them, she mumbled, "I don't know about this."

"Ignore them. Besides, they know you're American and they give you'll a break."

Before she could protest, he led her off. It was intoxicating, this dancing as a couple. Despite the few missteps, she soon found herself having a good time. After a few sets, when they were both out of breath, they returned to the table, sat down with relief, and reached for their drinks.

They stayed until the pub closed and were some of the last people to leave. On the ride back to the manor, the earl asked, "Did you enjoy yourself, Rachel?"

She nodded enthusiastically. "I loved it."

"They have dancing there every Sunday night. We could go if you'd like," he suggested casually.

"Oh, that's not necessary," she protested. He didn't have to go through all that trouble just to impress the public.

He laughed. "You're looking at me with a kind of horror on your face. Am I that bad of a dancer? Did my deodorant fail me?"

She laughed. "No, of course not. I just don't want you to feel obligated to take me dancing."

He shrugged. "I don't feel obligated. In fact, I enjoyed myself as well."

And so, it was sorted: Thomas and Rachel would go dancing in the village on Sunday nights.

Rachel gazed out the window, content. But she reminded herself that she was going home at the first of the year, and not to get used to being in the earl's arms every Sunday night.

CHAPTER TWELVE

T HOMAS STOOD AT RACHEL'S desk. He fingered a gold-embossed invitation and laid it in front of her. Mrs. Maher was out on an errand.

"There's that party up in Kildare. It's for charity, really. I meant to remind you of it earlier, but it slipped my mind. It's this Saturday."

Rachel picked up the invite and scanned it.

"The host is somewhat of a boor," Thomas said, thinking of Teddy Stabler. The last thing he wanted to do was inflict the idiot on Rachel.

"And you need to show your face," Rachel said, filling in the blanks.

"I do," he said.

"Would you like me to go with you?" she asked, and then added quickly, "For appearances' sake and all that." That was exactly what he wanted. If she'd go with him, it would not only look good, but he was guaranteed to pass an otherwise painful evening pleasurably. This new thought startled him. Was he looking forward to being with her? Just to be with her?

He'd have to give that some thought later. "If it's not too much trouble," he said.

She shook her head with a smile. "Not at all. I'll just need to make note of the date." Rachel pulled out a ledger that had the word "Diary" embossed in gold letters on the cover.

She began flipping through pages.

"You can keep the invitation."

She looked up at him with a smile. "That's fine." With a pen, she marked down the date on her calendar. It was amazing to him how she looked so natural in the manor. How it appeared as if she'd been there for years. All along.

From her desk drawer, she pulled out a letter and handed it to him.

"What's this?" he asked.

"It's a letter from the Glenbourne Historical Society," she replied. "They're having an open house at the end of February. They'd like to borrow some items to display for their feature on the history of the manor and the village." She looked up to the earl with a searching look on her face.

He was appreciative of the fact that she had at least told him before she had gone and donated the manor or something like that. "Why don't you handle that? What could we give them?"

She looked at him but didn't say anything.

He was thoughtful for a moment. "Actually, there are boxes somewhere in the manor with photos taken in the late nineteenth century. My great-grandmother was an American, and she loved photography. It was so new back then," he mused.

"I think that would be a wonderful idea," Rachel said.

"I'll have Percy or Mrs. Brennan locate the boxes and bring them down for you to sift through," Thomas said.

Rachel appeared to hesitate and then said, "Actually, Thomas, I'd rather not, if it's all the same."

"Really?" he asked, unable to hide his surprise. "I thought you'd be interested in something like this." It had her name written all over it.

She looked away. "I won't be here in February. So there really is no sense in me getting involved in a long-term project."

"Oh, right," he said. That hadn't occurred to him. He was so used to her being there that he couldn't imagine the manor without her.

Neither spoke, and he finally said, "I'd better get back to work."

Sammy appeared one evening as they had just sat down for dinner. He was grinning from ear to ear as he entered the room. He clapped his hands and headed toward Rachel, pulling her up from her chair and enveloping her in a bear hug. Thomas felt a bit jealous.

Rachel, caught off guard by the display of affection, laughed.

"Rachel, I can't thank you enough," Sammy gushed. "Your idea of a grand gesture worked." He held up his hand, showing off a wedding band on his ring finger. Thomas's eyes widened in surprise. Rachel's hands flew to her mouth, and she gasped.

"We wondered what had happened to you," Thomas said, standing up and congratulating his best friend. "There's been total radio silence from you."

"I took Trish to Paris," Sammy said. His smile disappeared for only an instant. "She took some coaxing in the beginning, but it all worked out in the end." He turned to Rachel and said, "Trish has always spoken about going away to Paris; she thought it was romantic. My Trish loves romance."

"This is wonderful," Rachel beamed. "I'm so happy for you."

"Yeah, me, too," Sammy confessed. "I flew her to Paris. Booked the bridal suite at an expensive Parisian hotel and popped the question at a little café with roses, champagne, and a violinist."

Rachel sighed. "It sounds so romantic."

"It was, it absolutely was," Sammy said. "We had such a great time, I asked her to marry me before we even left Paris."

Rachel clasped her hands together. "That's wonderful, Sammy. I'm so happy for you."

"Thanks, Rachel, you're a mate. If it weren't for you, I'd never have realized all that Trish meant to me and how to win her back," he said sincerely. "It sounds trite, but Trish truly is my soul mate."

Thomas looked at his wife, wondering what kind of grand gesture she'd like.

The last thing Thomas wanted to do was to go to this party of Teddy Stabler's. He found Teddy boorish on the best of days and downright insulting on the worst of them. He knew that Teddy referred to him as a half-breed behind his back because his great-grandfather had married an American.

Rachel chatted amiably on the drive up to Kildare. In their time together, her sunny disposition had shone through; she always seemed determined to make the best of things. He could not ask for anything more from her. It was nothing short of magnanimous. She had managed to turn his life upside down in the same way he had done with hers. The only difference was, he'd hand her a real-life divorce for the new year. He closed his eyes and groaned at what he had done to her life.

"Are you all right?" she asked from her side of the car.

Concern etched her face. He would have liked to get to know her better. What she thought of and what her dreams were. He was pretty sure a marriage of convenience and living in a foreign country with a stranger hadn't been at the top of her list of life goals and aspirations.

"I'm fine, just thinking," he said, giving her a reassuring smile.

She nodded and left him alone.

He felt compelled to speak. If only to make some conversation with her.

"This is one of those functions you have to attend, even though you don't really want to," he explained.

She laughed. He noticed that came easy to her. "It's called being an adult."

Even he had to laugh. "Yes, I guess it is. We won't stay long."

"I'll be fine. I googled Teddy Stabler. Apparently, he has an extensive art and porcelain collection."

The earl smiled at his wife. "Well, maybe if you play your cards right, he'll show it to you."

She batted her eyelashes and pretended to be coy. For a moment, Thomas was alarmed. He knew of Teddy's reputation. As far as women were concerned, he was a cad and a bounder.

He looked over at her again. He certainly didn't want to hand her over on a plate to Teddy. "Whatever you do, promise me you won't let him get you alone."

Rachel tilted her head and smiled. "Trish already gave me the lowdown on Teddy."

The earl still wasn't convinced. "In fact, I'll ask him if I can show you the collection myself."

"That really isn't necessary. I can manage," she said.

He said nothing but made a note to himself to pay attention to where Teddy was all evening in relation to Rachel.

As they entered the front hall of Teddy Stabler's mansion, Sammy was shrugging on his coat, grinning. Rachel thought marriage agreed with him. In any event, it had all worked out. Thank goodness, she thought.

"Leaving already?" Thomas asked, eying his friend.

Sammy acknowledged them with a nod. "I was here for thirty minutes, just enough to have a glass of champagne, circle the room once, say hello, and make a sizeable donation." He winked at Rachel. "I need to get home to my bride."

And before they could even say goodbye, he disappeared out the door.

Rachel supposed her preconceived ideas about Teddy Stabler colored her opinion of him. But even if she hadn't been given an earful about him, she soon learned that he was somewhat arrogant and crass and vulgar. Some of the things he said made her cringe.

When he slipped his arm around her, she deftly moved away, but Thomas stepped in.

"Now, Teddy," the earl said, placing his own arm protectively around Rachel's waist. "Get your own wife. You can't have mine."

"You don't share, Thomas," Teddy said with a pique of annoyance.

The earl made light of it. "Well, definitely not my wife."

He kept his arm around her waist. Although she was starting to get used to it, it still disconcerted her. Every time he touched her, her body reacted the same way: her heart rate picked up and she felt jittery, as if she were on fire. She looked up at him and searched his face. In return, he smiled at her. "Are you all right?"

She nodded.

"Teddy, would you mind if I showed Rachel your porcelain collection?" he asked.

Teddy made a face. "I would much rather show her myself."

"Humor me," the earl said with a slight edge in his voice. "After all, we are newlyweds."

Their host's eyes raked over Rachel's body in a manner that made her feel uncomfortable. Thomas pulled her tighter to him.

"That is a pity, my lord, but as you wish." Teddy made a slight bow.

Thomas whisked her out of the room to an adjoining one. Rachel looked around at the room, her mouth falling open. It was a high-ceilinged room with red silk wallpaper, dark wood furniture and hints of gold, bronze, and red. The hardwood floor was covered with a luxurious Persian carpet, and glass display units stood on gleaming walnut pedestals. Rachel gasped at the size of Teddy's Chinese porcelain collection.

Rachel recognized items from the Ming dynasty, a type of porcelain that was quite difficult to obtain these days. She looked around and thought of the fortune represented in just this room alone.

"This is crazy," Rachel whispered. "Do you know the value of all this porcelain?" Thomas nodded. "I have an idea. Teddy is a serious art collector. It's good to know he has one redeeming quality."

"Only one?" She giggled.

The earl raised his eyebrows, leaned into her, and whispered, "It's the only one I can find so far."

They spent the next thirty minutes looking at the various pieces, huddled together, whispering, and Rachel thought it was amongst the best thirty minutes she had ever spent. They agreed that a fifteenth-century holy water vessel, inspired by the ones used by Tibetan Buddhist monks, was their favorite piece. It was sublime.

"Come on, let's go and say our goodbyes," Thomas said. He took Rachel's hand and guided her through the door. She got another thrill as he held her hand, leading the way out of this place. She was more than ready to leave, as well. More than anything, she wanted to be alone with him.

They slipped through to the next room. Teddy was entertaining a group of friends and by their raucous laughter, he must have been very amusing. Their host had his back to them. As the others in the group eyed them, the laughter came to an abrupt halt, but the host kept talking.

"The Earls of Glenbourne have always had a fancy for the Americans. The current earl is a mixed breed himself. Though why the fascination with the Yanks, I do not know. The new wife does not inspire, does she? Not a great beauty, that's for sure. But still, I'd like to see what's under all those clothes."

Rachel froze as she realized she was the topic of conversation, and a not a very nice one, either. She looked over to Thomas, who had dropped her hand. A scowl had replaced the smile, and his face was a mask of thunder and fury.

But Teddy Stabler still had not copped on to their presence. "I mean, she must be a volcano in—"

Before Rachel could lay her hand on the earl to restrain him, he was gone. He spun Teddy around, and the look of surprise on the host's face was accompanied by a collective gasp from the crowd gathered around him. The earl's fist landed on Teddy's chin and sent the shocked host reeling back, tottering on his feet. But the second punch landed right across his nose, and the result was both a crunching noise and an immediate gush of blood. Teddy fell back on the floor.

Thomas Yates, now breathless, stood over his host, who covered his nose with his hands as blood seeped between his fingers.

"I don't care what you say about me or that you insult me. But don't you ever disparage my wife again." He spat on the ground next to him. "Ever."

No one said a word. No one helped the host off the ground.

The earl turned his head to one side, stretched his shoulders, and pulled down the sleeves of his suit coat. He turned toward Rachel, and his features softened at the sight of her. "I'm ready to go home. Are you?"

"I am, Thomas," she said.

He held out his hand, she laid hers in his, and they walked out together.

The drive home from Kildare was quiet. The only words uttered were Thomas's apology as soon as they climbed into the car. The wonderful companionship they'd shared as they viewed the porcelain collection had been shattered by their host's insults and the ensuing violence. Thomas didn't know who he was angrier with: Teddy for his crude remarks, or himself for losing control of his temper. But he'd do it all over again if he had to. Rachel was his wife, and he wanted to protect her. Several times, he looked over at her, but she stared straight ahead out the window. He didn't know what she was feeling:

anger, hurt, or all of the above. He wasn't one for fighting, never had been, but Teddy had gone too far. And the earl had to admit to a bit of satisfaction at being the one to close Teddy's mouth, if only for a few minutes.

When they arrived home, they walked silently up the stairs.

They went to their respective rooms to get ready for bed. He knew he could beg off and tell Rachel that he'd sleep in his own bed, but he was too afraid that she'd let him. And the thing was, over the past few weeks he had gotten used to sleeping in the same room with her. It amazed him. He had slept alone for years and had figured it would take time to get used to sleeping with another person. But to him, it felt like he and Rachel had been sharing a room for years.

After he washed his hands and brushed his teeth, he put on his pajama bottoms and a T-shirt and threw on his bathrobe. He knocked on the connecting door, but there was no answer. He knocked again and frowned. Maybe she was angry. He opened the door and called out, "Rachel?"

Entering her room, he glanced around, but there was no sign of her. The door to the adjoining bathroom was open, and the light was off.

A quick look around told him that her things were still there and she hadn't fled in the middle of the night. He found himself relieved at that.

His eyes wandered over to the chaise. It had been quite comfortable when he was five, but not so much thirty years later. He'd been waking up in the mornings with his back stiff and his joints aching.

And tonight, when he had thrown that second punch, he'd felt something give in his lower back. Not to mention his hand was now bruised and swollen.

A candy wrapper on the floor by Rachel's side of the bed caught his attention. He bent over to pick it up, noticing something had fallen between the bed and nightstand. He slid his fingers between the two pieces of furniture and pulled out a calendar. Frowning, he studied it. On each of the days that had passed was an X in thick, black marker. He flipped ahead and saw that she had circled December 30th and written the word "home" in big letters in the center of the circle. He folded it back to the current date and put it back where he'd found it. Its existence raised a lot of questions in his mind. Was she that unhappy at the manor? Did she really miss her family that much? Was she that homesick? Was pretending to be his wife, with everything at her disposal, that much of a sacrifice? Apparently, it was.

Before he could muse further on the subject, the door opened and Rachel entered, already in her pajamas and that heavy robe that must have weighed a ton. She held up a bag of ice and smiled. "I thought you could use some ice for your hand."

He felt himself relax, and he walked over to the chaise and sat down. When Rachel sat down next to him, her leg brushed against his, giving him a thrill. He looked quickly up at her. She seemed unaware of the effect she had on him. But of course, how could she be aware of how he felt when she was counting the days until she went home?

"You seem a bit stiff," she noted as she took his hand in hers and placed the bag of ice over it.

He winced. "It's my back. I may have been a bit too eager with the punches I threw."

"I can imagine."

Her hands were feminine and soft. The simple gold wedding band he had placed on her finger weeks ago looked as if it belonged there.

"Are you hurt?" she asked.

He looked over at her and smiled. She had such a pretty face. "No. Are you?"

She shook her head. "No."

A silence fell between them. Thomas attempted to bridge it. He wanted no awkwardness from him to her; she was too lovely and didn't deserve it.

"I am so very sorry for what happened tonight. Teddy's insults and my reaction. I could have behaved more like a gentleman."

She shrugged. "It's all right."

He looked at her sharply. "No, it is not all right. I don't usually go around throwing punches."

She sighed. "What I mean is that he is right; after all, I am kind of a plain Jane."

"You are not!" he said, surprised at his own vehemence.

She looked at him with a knowing look, raised one eyebrow and said, "Even you once said I wasn't worth a second look."

He closed his eyes and groaned at his own shame. "And I truly regret I made those untrue remarks. Please have pity on the poor, stupid fool who uttered them."

She laughed and when he looked at her, he saw that her eyes were clear and bright. "When you put it like that, I am moved to pity, and all is forgiven."

He was mesmerized by her. He was tempted to tell her that he wanted to give her a second look, and a third look, and thousands of looks, but he held back. She might not want to hear that. She might view it as insincere.

She stood up. "Between your hand and your back, you're not going to be very comfortable on the chaise."

He prayed she didn't banish him to his room.

"Come on, Rocky, you can sleep on the other half of the bed. It's big enough for the two of us," she said.

He sat there, stunned. She glanced over her shoulder and said, "And if you should try anything funny, just know that I'm a southpaw."

He smiled, stood up, and followed her to the bed.

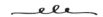

When the earl climbed into bed bedside her, Rachel's heart raced. She held her breath as she listened to him getting comfortable on his side of the bed. He was so close she could reach out and touch him. And he smelled heavenly.

Stealing a quick glance at him, she saw that he had his hands clasped behind his head on the pillow. He stared at the ceiling.

Secretly, she had been pleased when he punched Teddy Stabler. Although she abhorred violence, she had felt humiliated at the time. Immediately, without a thought, the earl had jumped to her defense. It was the only thing she had thought about on the way home.

"Rachel, can I ask you something?" he asked in the dark, turning toward her. "Something personal."

She hesitated, guarded. He was in her bed now. She supposed it was all right. "Okay."

"It has to do with your conditions on the contract," he said. "I'm curious."

"Curious about what?"

"About your why," he replied.

"Oh," she said. It was a personal question. Finally, she said, "If I tell you, do you promise not to laugh?"

"I give you my word," he whispered.

She hadn't known Thomas long, but what she did know was that he was a man of honor.

She cleared her throat. "I haven't had much luck with past boyfriends. Not that I've had many, but the few I've had haven't worked out."

"I'm sorry to hear that," he said.

"There's a girl at work who has this amazing boyfriend—he's always doing nice things for her," she explained.

"And your boyfriends have not done nice things for you," he said.

"It's not that. They just weren't the romantic type. None of them would know a grand gesture if it knocked them in the face," she said with a hint of exasperation. "And compliments or maybe cook me a dinner? I couldn't even get them to take me out for dinner."

"Really? Were they raised in caves?" Thomas asked.

Rachel laughed. "It would seem so."

They were both quiet for a moment. Rachel spoke first. "I know I used your desperation for leverage when I wrote out that contract, and I am sorry. I just wanted to know what it would feel like. To have a man treat you like you were worth something to him."

Thomas remained quiet. But when he spoke, he said, "Don't apologize, Rachel. And please promise me that you won't ever settle for less than you deserve."

"I promise, Thomas," she said.

"Besides," he said. "Paying you compliments and cooking dinners for you has been quite enjoyable for me."

Oh.

CHAPTER THIRTEEN

T HE EARL'S BACK IMPROVED with time, and his hand healed, but it was an unspoken agreement between them that Thomas would continue to sleep in Rachel's bed. They each respected the other's boundary and kept to their own sides. It was a large bed, and there was plenty of room for the both of them. When the lights were turned off and darkness enveloped the room, it encouraged a warmth and intimacy between them.

For the first few nights, neither said a word, and both were aware of the close proximity in which the other lay. Those first few nights, Rachel lay still, thinking things over. It was desperate, not to reach out for him. The image of him slugging Teddy Stabler replayed in her mind. In her life, she could never remember a man, other than her brothers, defending her like that.

By the fourth night, Rachel could no longer take the silence. "How was your day?" she whispered in the darkness.

"How was my day?" the earl repeated, a little surprised.

She let out a chuckle. "It seems like something a wife would ask."

"Yes, I suppose it is," he agreed.

She hoped he would keep talking; she liked the sound of his voice with his gentle accent in the dark. And his masculinity—it was hard not to think about the way his T-shirt stretched across his sculpted torso and biceps. More than once, she imagined running her hands along his chest and down his arms. The scent of his aftershave, too, was proving to be a distraction.

"My day was fine. Productive," he said.

"Do you like your work?"

"I do. I love the law," he explained. "You always know where you stand."

"Was your father a solicitor?" she asked.

"He was, but he didn't practice. My grandfather was a solicitor as well. He had a practice that he ran right here out of the manor. His clients were all villagers."

"What would his business involve? Wills and such?" she asked.

"Yes, mostly, or anything to do with the land. The villagers used to come to my grandfather for advice. Every Sunday, the doors were open and the villagers would queue up outside and wait their turn to see my grandfather. There would be tea and cake served all day," he said.

"What kind of advice would he have dispensed?"

"The usual stuff back then. So-and-so was thinking of buying this field, and what did he think about that? Was the drainage good enough or was it too rocky? Or one time, a couple came in and their first child had been born and remained nameless, the father wanting to name it after his own father, and the mother wanting to name it after hers. They couldn't agree."

"What did your grandfather do?" she asked.

"He put both names into a hat and pulled one out," he said, laughing at the memory of it. "He said it was the fairest way. I don't remember what name was chosen. All I remember was that the couple was so impressed they ended up naming the baby after my grandfather. Thomas."

"You're not serious!"

"I am."

They laughed together in the dark. The earl picked up his train of thought. "But after my grandfather died, the villagers stopped coming to the manor. My parents were rarely here, and I was away at school."

"That's too bad," she said.

Thomas agreed. "Especially for the older ones who really just came for a chat."

Jer came to Rachel's mind. There were ways to keep the old traditions alive and still put your own stamp on things. It took a long while for sleep to come to Rachel. Her mind raced with possibilities for the manor, the villagers, and most of all, Thomas. But how to convince him of his own destiny?

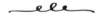

Rachel stood in the drawing room, looking out on the vast lawns. Rain pelted against the windows, and the afternoon sky was practically black. Despite it being early December, there was still no snow. Thomas had told her that there might be snow for Christmas. If not Christmas, then definitely January. It made her more homesick. She folded her arms across her chest to stave off the damp. She harbored mixed feelings about going home. But she was anxious about Christmas. The thought of being so far away from her family on the biggest day of the year made her sick. She stood at the window and started to cry. She pulled a tissue from her pocket, gave her nose a good blow, wiped it, and put the tissue away.

"Ugh!" she muttered in frustration.

Thomas entered the room and looked around. "How's it going with the decorating?"

They both looked at the freshly cut twelve-foot Douglas fir that had been brought in the previous day. Decorations and ornaments that had been part of the Glenbourne family for decades lay in boxes scattered around the tree. She'd made no headway. She turned around and gave him a smile, not sure if she was trying to convince him or herself.

He looked alarmed. "Have you been crying?"

"It's nothing," she said, giving him a weak smile.

"Crying is never nothing," he said. He stepped closer to her and she stepped back. She couldn't bear it if he touched her. She would surely start crying again. From need. And want. She looked up at him and saw warmth and concern in his eyes. Unfortunately, it started the tears again. Had he been mean or impatient, it would have put an end to her tears right away.

"Please tell me," he pleaded. "What has upset you? Has someone been unkind to you?"

She shook her head. "Oh no, everyone has been wonderful. It's just that . . . " Her voice trailed off, and she looked out the window, thinking of home and snow covering the ground, and her parents and brothers and nieces and nephew.

"It's just what?" he repeated, attempting to draw it out of her.

"I love Christmas," she started, looking wistfully off into the distance.

He said nothing, waiting for her to finish.

Bowing her head, she said quietly, "I miss my family."

"I can only imagine, and yet here you are stuck at the manor with me," he said.

She laughed. "I wouldn't say I'm stuck. It's just that Christmas is a family holiday, and one likes to be with one's family."

"Is there anything I can do to make it more palatable for you?" he asked. "To help you get through it?"

She smiled and shook her head. "It's only one day."

"Would you like to go home?" he asked.

Immediately, she waved away the idea. "No, I'll stay here."

"Would you like to plan a Christmas dinner? Something you would normally do in the States? We could invite Sammy and Trish," he said.

She was overwhelmed by his desire to make the holiday easier for her, and that touched her to the depths of her soul. Her tears disappeared and she felt better. She reached out and laid her hand on his arm. "Thank you for being so kind. I will think of something, if that's all right with you."

"Anything, Rachel. Anything you'd like."

"What do you usually do?" she asked.

"When my parents were alive, we spent Christmas here at the manor with my grandfather. Christmas morning, we'd have a big breakfast, and then dinner was served at seven. Turkey and ham, of course. On St. Stephen's Day, we had a luncheon of smoked salmon and champagne."

"It sounds wonderful!" she said. "Do you still do all that?"

He shook his head. "No, it seems pointless just for me. I have some cousins that I usually go to for Christmas dinner."

She thought it sounded a little sad, and ideas began to take shape in her head. "Are you planning on going to your cousin's this year?"

He shook his head and said thoughtfully, "No, because I hoped we'd do something here."

Something about the way he said that touched her. The use of the pronoun "we" and all the togetherness it implied. She didn't want to get her hopes up, but the black cloud that had surrounded her began to lift.

The earl looked toward the tree. "There's no rush to decorate the tree, really, Rachel, and if you prefer, I can always have staff do it."

"Oh, no!" she protested. "It wouldn't be personal if the family didn't decorate it."

"Will I help you then?" he asked.

"That would be nice," she said. "Do you have time?"

He nodded. "I can spare an hour."

Feeling energized, she headed toward the boxes with purpose and determination. She began to lift the lids off the boxes. There were some exquisite ornaments.

They decorated the Christmas tree, and Thomas held the ladder while Rachel climbed it and placed the star on top. He was eye-level with her legs and saw that they were quite shapely. He redirected his attention from her legs and from the thoughts he was having about the rest of her. Looking up at her, he was moved by how earnest she looked, trying to get the star centered.

Mrs. Brennan brought tea and scones just as Rachel was descending the ladder. She nodded toward the tree. "It's looking very pretty, Lady Glenbourne."

Rachel smiled at her. Thomas had noted that since the housekeeper had returned from her visit with her sister, she hadn't been as surly.

"It's a beautiful tree," Rachel pronounced. She buttered a scone, put a bit of jam on it, handed it Thomas, and then fixed one for herself. She poured tea into cups, and he watched as she fixed his tea the way he liked it: just a dash of milk. But he knew how she took her tea, as well: one spoonful of sugar and a good bit of milk.

He had to agree with her. Christmas was a magical time. As a child, his Christmases at the manor had been full of fun and traditions. He'd walk the grounds with his grandfather, who was always decked out in tweeds, and then they'd go to the village, where his grandfather would stop for a pint. And that meant a bag of sweets for himself. His grandfather was always talking to the villagers. In many ways, he was truly one of them.

"You are deep in thought, Lord Glenbourne," Rachel observed.

"Am I? Just thinking of my grandfather," he said.

"You miss him?" she asked over the rim of her teacup as she sipped her tea.

He nodded, sipping his own. "I was an only grandchild. He had an amazing influence on my life," he said.

They went quiet, both lost in their thoughts.

Thomas placed his plate and teacup on the table. "I must get back to work."

Rachel sat up straighter. "Oh, all right."

He left her and headed back to the study to conduct some business. The image of Rachel crying earlier had not left his mind. It bothered him that she was so upset.

A plan began to form, and his mood lifted. He pulled up their contract on his computer, nodding to himself as he reviewed the particulars of their business arrangement, the details of his plan solidifying in his mind. He reached for his phone and dialed a number.

After Thomas had left, Rachel finished decorating, but then she noticed some more boxes along the wall. She glanced over at the tree, which was now fully decorated, and didn't think there was room for one more ornament.

Lifting the lid on one of the boxes, she saw that it was filled with photo albums and loose pictures and postcards, as was the second box and the third one.

She settled down on the floor and made herself comfortable. She began to sift through them, getting lost in the pictures of the previous generations. There were a lot of pictures of Thomas as a little boy, and he had been adorable. He was photographed with his parents, his grandfather, and a dog, an Irish Wolfhound like Max.

She was there for over two hours, lost in the history of the manor and its residents.

Rachel bundled up against the damp weather in her coat, scarf, and gloves. She looped her purse over her shoulder, along with a canvas bag holding a container of homemade chicken-vegetable soup, courtesy of Mrs. Shortt, and some rolls. When she hadn't seen Jer around the village, her enquiries had informed her that he had been laid up with the flu. She planned to drop off some soup and make sure he was all right.

As she was exiting the manor, Thomas appeared, similarly dressed.

"Where are you heading off to, Rachel?" he asked.

She lifted the canvas bag. "I'm taking some soup over to Jer. I heard he's been sick."

"I'm on my way to Dublin, so I can drop you off," he said.

She frowned. "I don't want to hold you up."

"Not at all," he said. "There's plenty of time. Let me take that." He removed the canvas bag from her grasp.

"Thank you," she said.

They got into his BMW and buckled up. The blast of warm air from the heater felt good. Rachel shivered. The earl looked over at her and said with concern, "It will warm up after a bit."

She smiled to reassure him. "It's just the damp; I don't know if I could ever get used to it."

He grimaced. "I know."

They both went silent, Rachel thinking that that was something she didn't have to worry about: getting used to the damp. She wouldn't be there long. And somehow that thought made her miserable.

The sight of the village as they drove into town never grew old to Rachel. It was so pretty with the cottages and shops painted in their vibrant colors, and the thatched roofs with their intricate designs, which were the signature of the thatcher. Rachel had learned that thatching was a dying art, and that was a shame. Heritage and history and where you came from were so important.

But now the village was all decorated for Christmas. Giant wreaths with great red bows hung from the black lampposts. Strings of white lights spanned the main thoroughfare and Christmas displays adorned shop windows. Holiday music, piped in from speakers, floated through the village and gave the atmosphere a festive feel. It was hard not to get caught up in it.

Thomas managed to find a spot right in front of Jer's home. It was a sleepy village, and things didn't really come to life until ten in the morning. It was one of the things Rachel found that she loved about rural Ireland: the laid-back atmosphere. Sundays were amazingly quiet on the roads, especially early in the morning. It was something she could definitely get used to.

As she climbed out of the car, Rachel turned to Thomas. "Would you like to come in and say hello?"

Thomas shook his head. "Another time. I've got to get to Dublin."

"Of course," she conceded, unable to hide her disappointment. "Have a safe trip."

"I'll be back by the end of the week," he said.

Rachel stood on the pavement for a moment, watching him until his car disappeared. She couldn't understand why he was so reluctant to get involved with the villagers. She had hoped to make a difference before she left, but with less than a month to go, there just wasn't enough time. Thomas was a tough nut to crack; it would take a lifetime, which she didn't have.

With her canvas bag full of food, she approached Jer's front door. She was worried about him. She hadn't seen him in a while, and when she had tried ringing his landline the day before, there had been no answer.

Jer's home was located in a row of terraced housing, each space sharing a common wall on either side. These groupings contained various shops, pubs, and private homes. On the roofs remained the chimneys, in clusters of four directly over a common wall.

Jer's house shared common walls with the pub on its left and a beauty salon on the right. It was painted the color of a waffle, with a brown door. There was a single window next to the door, and two windows on the second floor. White lace curtains hung in all the windows.

Rachel looked up toward the upstairs windows and hoped he was all right.

Once again, as she rang the bell, she wished Thomas would take a bit more interest in the welfare of the people around him. Namely, his staff and the villagers. It was there, she was sure; it just needed to be teased out of him.

Rachel frowned and rang the bell again. When there was no answer, she leaned down, opened the letterbox slotted in the door, and called through, "Jer!"

There was a weak "Aye" from somewhere in the back of the house.

Relieved, she tried the door handle, and it sprang open. She stepped inside, into a long, narrow hall. To the left was a parlor that looked as if it hadn't been used in years. The furnishings appeared dated, but the room was tidy.

At the end of the hall was a door that led to a cozy kitchen with a large window looking out over a small but well-kept back garden. There was an open fire in the fireplace on the other side of the room which was currently in full blaze. In one of the two chairs by the fire sat Jer, his hair going off in all directions, wearing a brown dressing gown over striped pajamas.

"Lady Glenbourne, what are you doing here?" Jer asked in surprise, sitting up in his chair.

Rachel sat down and folded her hands in her lap. Jer didn't look so well.

"You haven't been around for a while, and I became concerned," Rachel said.

Jer shrugged. "I've been laid up." Right on cue, he started coughing, his face turning red. "If I'd known you were coming, I would have gotten dressed."

"Oh, don't worry about that," Rachel said. "Have you seen a doctor?"

"No, I don't think it's necessary," Jer said in between coughs.

"How long have you been sick?" Rachel asked.

"A little over a week," he said.

"Have you been eating?"

"Not today," Jer said. "Don't have the energy."

Rachel stood up. "I've brought some soup. How about a small bowl? Just to eat something."

Jer smiled. "That would be nice."

"And then I'm going to ring for the doctor."

Jer went to protest but thought better of it and then reluctantly agreed.

Rachel looked around the kitchen, found a small pot for the soup, and went about heating it on the stove. After locating the toaster, she popped in a slice of bread to make toast. She filled the kettle and turned it on. As she fixed Jer's meal, she could hear him coughing incessantly.

Rachel placed the bowl of soup and the toast on the table beside Jer. She waited until he had eaten a few spoonfuls before heading to the phone.

"Now who is your GP? Sullivan or Leahy?"

"Why Sullivan of course! I wouldn't give that other one houseroom," the older man said vehemently.

Rachel chuckled and took the liberty of browsing through the telephone book by the landline, and soon found the number she was looking for. After a chat with the receptionist, she hung up the phone and said, "The doctor will be out on his lunch hour."

"All right," Jer said with resignation in his voice. He slowly ladled soup into his mouth.

As he ate, she went around the small house, cleaning up.

Rachel stayed for a while to make sure he was going to be all right. When he finished eating, Rachel removed the dishes and washed them up in the sink, dried them, and put them away.

Jer glanced over at Rachel, a look of horror on his face. "It isn't right, the Countess of Glenbourne washing up my ware."Rachel smiled at him. "I don't mind."

Once the few pieces of ware were dried and put away, and after she set a hot cup of tea next to him, Rachel pulled on her coat.

"I'll check on you tomorrow," she said.

"Lady Glenbourne, that is not necessary," the older man protested.

"It is," Rachel said. "You need to eat. To keep up your strength."

"I'm certainly no match for ye," Jer said with a twinkle in his eye.

Rachel laughed and, satisfied that he was in better shape than when she'd arrived, she left, remembering to leave the door unlocked for the doctor.

CHAPTER FOURTEEN

T HOMAS WOULD BE IN Dublin for the rest of the week, so Rachel was left to her own devices. She had only three weeks left before she returned home, and she had mixed feelings about that. One day after lunch, she went to the village to check on Jer and made a stop at the library to talk to Marian. Even though she had the manor library at her disposal, she still liked to hang out in the village and talk to people. And despite the librarian being closer to her mother's age, the two of them had hit it off.

As she got ready to head back to the manor, the librarian asked her, "Excuse me, Lady Glenbourne, but are you feeling all right? It's just that you look a bit pale."

Rachel shrugged it off. "That time of year." Jer came to mind, and she added, "There's a lot of stuff going around."

"Mind yourself," Marian cautioned as they bid each other goodbye.

Rachel had walked into the village that morning and now she was regretting that decision. But she began the trek back. It was only a couple of miles. She had taken to walking into the village on the nice days when there was no threat of rain. The exercise was good, and it allowed her to think. It also compensated for all the candy she ate.

But the librarian was right; she did not feel well. She soldiered on, her purse slung over her shoulder. She was polite to villagers as she passed by, but she was anxious about getting back to the manor. She oscillated between severe shivers and the feeling of being overheated to the point where she wanted to remove her coat. Her mouth felt parched. She knew she could ring the manor and have someone pick her up, but she didn't want to bother anyone.

It was great relief she felt when she arrived at the manor gate. She had never been so happy to be somewhere in her whole life. Only about half a mile to go. Then she was going to take a shower, get back into her pajamas, take some Tylenol, and go to bed. Her legs felt heavy, and the midday December sun beat down on her brow. She felt as if she were in the tropics. Panting, she soon crested the hill, and when the manor came into sight, she let out a squeak of joy, for that was all she could manage. She'd no sooner done that than she began to retch and, standing in the grass, she brought up all the remnants of her lunch. She was desperate to hurry back to the manor and the privacy of her bedroom, but her legs felt weak and her stomach felt like it was a competing gymnast at the summer Olympics. She only managed a few more steps before her stomach revolted and she felt compelled to vomit again. When she was finished heaving, she pulled a tissue from her coat pocket and wiped her mouth. A sheen of perspiration appeared on her forehead.

The manor didn't appear to be getting any closer, as she kept having to stop and retch. Once her stomach was emptied of its contents, she continued to retch and heave, bringing up only bile. Exhausted and drained, she collapsed on the wet grass, thinking she'd just close her eyes for a moment.

The colors were vibrant in her dreams and at some point, a voice that sounded very far away exclaimed, "Lady Glenbourne!" She recognized it as Laura's. She tried to stand with the housemaid's help, but as soon as she was upright, she began heaving.

"Come on, let's get you into the car and back to the manor," Laura said.

Rachel shook her head. "No, not without a bucket." The thought of throwing up in someone's car mortified her; it upset her more than the vomiting itself.

"It's all right, Lady Glenbourne, I don't mind if you throw up in my car," Laura said, sounding as if she was trying to convince herself.

Between retches, Rachel managed a chuckle. "Yes, but I do."

They were distracted by one of the gardeners whizzing by them in a golf cart.

Laura flagged him down, and he circled back. "Lady Glenbourne has taken ill," she informed him.

The gardener jumped down. "Come on, Countess, let's get you back to the manor."

"I need a bucket," Rachel said, her stomach coiling again. She gasped.

"Not at all," he said, getting under one of her arms while the maid got under the other. "If you think you're going to get sick, just hang your head over the side."

Rachel slumped on the backseat of the golf cart with Laura beside her.

"I am so sorry for all the trouble I've caused," Rachel said. The cart rolled into motion and Rachel's stomach rebelled violently. Embarrassed, she hung her head over the side of the cart, throwing up onto the grass.

"Don't worry about it," he said.

They were at the front steps of the manor within minutes, but Rachel refused to get out of the golf cart and step into the manor without a bucket. There was no way she was going to make a mess all over the place for someone else to clean up. Laura ran inside and returned within minutes with Mrs. Brennan at her side and a bucket in her hand.

"What happened?" Mrs. Brennan asked, alarmed.

"As I was leaving, I found her on the side of the road, sick," Laura explained.

"All right, take her up to her room," Mrs. Brennan instructed. Rachel could hear the housekeeper issuing commands. "Percy, ring for the doctor at once. In the meantime, I'll ring Lord Glenbourne. Jim, would you help Laura in getting Lady Glenbourne upstairs?"

Rachel was relieved that someone else was in charge. She wanted to just give in to the blackness. With the gardener on one side and the maid on the other, they managed to get her up the staircase and to her room. The gardener had the bucket looped over one arm. She felt herself being set gently on her bed and was aware of the voice of Laura, thanking the gardener.

Rachel heard water running in the en suite bathroom and then felt a cool cloth pressed against her forehead.

"Shh, Lady Glenbourne," Laura said soothingly. "We're going to take care of you; don't you worry. We're going to take care of you like you've been taking care of all of us."

Rachel groaned again. She heard the door to her room open and from far away, she heard the housekeeper's voice. She hoped Mrs. Brennan wouldn't give out. Rachel just didn't have the energy within her to battle her.

"The doctor will be here soon," Mrs. Brennan said. She placed her hand on Rachel's forehead. "She's on fire!"

There was the sound of cabinet and wardrobe doors being opened, and the last thing Rachel heard was the voice of Mrs. Brennan. "Lady Glenbourne," she said softly. "We need to get you out of these damp clothes. We're going to put your nightgown on you."

Rachel agreed weakly. There was the sour smell of vomit on her clothes. She stood up from the bed, wobbly, and stripped down to her bra and panties. Mrs. Brennan helped her into her pajamas. Laura put her discarded clothes in a plastic bag for the laundry.

"I need to use the bathroom," Rachel said. She wanted to brush her teeth and wash her face.

"Of course," Mrs. Brennan said. Both the maid and the housekeeper walked her to the bathroom. Although Rachel felt weak, she didn't think that was necessary. Fortunately, neither insisted on going into the bathroom with her. Once finished, she emerged feeling a bit fresher but exhausted. She sat down on her side of the bed and slid her legs under the blanket. The housekeeper pulled the blankets up for Rachel.

"How is your sister doing?" Rachel asked.

"She has a long road ahead of her, but she's going to be fine," Mrs. Brennan replied. "Now don't worry about her. Just get some rest, Lady Glenbourne."

Rachel decided to follow the housekeeper's instructions. But she sat up and Mrs. Brennan looked at her, concerned.

"Please, Mrs. Brennan, make sure you all wash your hands well," she said, not wanting to get anyone else sick.

Thomas had no recollection of the drive from Dublin back to the manor. Coming out of a meeting late afternoon, he'd been alarmed to find three missed calls from home. When he'd heard the anxious voice of his housekeeper on the voicemail, telling him that Rachel had fallen ill, he told his secretary that he had an emergency back home and needed to leave. It was only when he was in his car that he called the manor. In his lifetime, he could never remember his housekeeper ever ringing him on his phone. When she told him they'd found Rachel on the side of the road, vomiting, he stepped harder on the gas pedal.

She assured him that the doctor was on his way. Thomas thought that if Mrs. Brennan was worried about Rachel, then it must be pretty bad.

It was dark by the time he rolled through the gates of his estate.

As he approached the manor, he saw that for the most part it was shrouded in darkness. There were no lights on in the downstairs windows, only a faint light upstairs from the window of Rachel's bedroom. He glanced up at that and wished her to be well.

He pushed through the front door and was immediately struck by the fact that the atmosphere of the manor had changed since he'd left the other day. There was one small light on in the grand hall, and the rest of the interior was hidden in shadows. But he did not miss the staff sitting on the steps of the grand staircase, quietly, waiting. As he headed for the staircase, he was approached by both Mrs. Brennan and Percy. Mrs. Brennan was all flustered, and even the usually unflappable Percy had a look of worry on his face.

"How is she?" Thomas asked.

Mrs. Brennan shook her head. "Lady Glenbourne's fever has gone higher. She's still vomiting. We rang for the doctor a second time. He's with her now. I've never seen anyone get so ill so quickly. She was fine this morning at breakfast."

"I'll go to her now," he said.

He took the stairs two at a time, aware of the staff's eyes on him. But this wasn't for show. This wasn't for pretend. He was worried sick about Rachel. He heard Mrs. Brennan say to Mrs. Shortt, "Let's get dinner ready for Lord Glenbourne and maybe make some tea for the rest of the staff. Take one of the housemaids to help you."

Thomas wanted to tell her not to bother, as his appetite had deserted him. Outside of Rachel's bedroom door, he drew in a deep breath before he entered. He stepped inside his wife's bedroom, immediately drawn to the figure on the bed. Rachel was dressed in her pajamas, her beautiful hair was matted around her hairline, and she was an awful shade of white. Thomas frowned. He sat on the edge of the bed and took her hand. It was hot, and that alarmed him.

At the other side of the room, the doctor stood near the window, speaking on his phone. Thomas returned his attention to his wife.

"Rachel?" he whispered.

Her eyes opened and her brow creased. "Thomas?" she asked in a whisper.

"I'm right here, Rachel," he said, trying to reassure her. Her forehead relaxed.

"You didn't have to leave work early, did you? I didn't want them to call you," she said anxiously.

"Shh, we finished early, and I was already on my way home," he lied. He didn't want her upset.

The doctor finished his call and stepped forward. "Lord Glenbourne?"

Thomas stood from the bed, nodded, and extended his hand. "Thomas Yates. How is she?"

"I'm Dr. Greene," the physician said, shaking the earl's hand. He nodded toward Rachel. "Lady Glenbourne seems to have a nasty stomach bug."

As if on cue, Rachel sat bolt upright, leaned over the side of the bed, grabbed the bucket, and retched into it.

Thomas immediately sat back down next to her and held back her hair.

In between heaves, Rachel groaned, "Oh, Thomas, don't touch me. I don't want you to get sick."

"Don't worry about me," he said with a smile. He turned to the doctor. "What is the plan?"

"The main thing is to keep her hydrated. I know it's difficult with vomiting but rest her stomach. Nothing solid. Start with flat 7-Up or Coke, then clear liquids as she can tolerate them."

"And if she doesn't stop vomiting?"

"She'll have to go into A & E."

Thomas did not like the sound of that. The A & E department was notoriously hellish due to the lack of beds and staff shortages. No, that wouldn't be good enough.

Rachel set the pail back on the floor. Thomas stood up and helped her back into bed and covered her with a blanket.

"What would be done at the hospital that couldn't be done here?" he asked.

The doctor shrugged. "At the very least, she'd need IV hydration."

"Can we do that here?" Thomas asked, running his hand through his hair.

"Yes, of course, but it will cost," the doctor started.

Thomas gave a dismissive wave of his hand, not taking his eyes off of Rachel. "Look, whatever it takes, whatever the cost. If it comes to that, I'd prefer to have her here at the manor. We can hire a nurse." he looked up to the doctor.

The doctor nodded, scribbling on a notepad. Tearing off a script, he handed it to Thomas. "Have this filled at the pharmacy in the village. I'll be back tomorrow to check on Lady Glenbourne."

"Thank you," Thomas said.

Dr. Greene closed up his medical bag and lifted it from the chaise. "We'll see how tonight goes. I'll be back in the morning." He paused and looked from Rachel to Thomas. "Is there any chance your wife might be pregnant?"

Embarrassed, Thomas said, "No, I don't think so."

"She should probably take a pregnancy test just to rule it out."

"I'll pick one up at the chemist," Thomas said. But he had no intention of doing that. There was no need. Unfortunately.

He walked the doctor to the door and thanked him.

As the doctor left, Max slipped in. He ran around to Rachel's side of the bed before Thomas could grab him. The dog whined and put his paws on the bed.

"Max, no," Thomas said in a low, stern voice.

The dog stepped down but continued to whine. Weakly, Rachel's arm lifted off the bed and settled on the dog's head. She patted him and he calmed down. "It's okay, Max."

Thomas took hold of his collar and said to the dog, "I know how you feel. But you can't stay in here."

"He can stay," Rachel said.

"No, he'll only be in the way," Thomas said and added quickly, knowing how she felt about the dog, "But I promise to bring him in regularly for visits."

She nodded and closed her eyes.

He opened the door and the dog trotted out with a downcast glance over his shoulder. The earl shut the door firmly behind him.

Alone with Rachel, Thomas pulled a chair right up next to the bed and sat down. Folding his arms and crossing his legs, he settled in for what he thought was going to be a long night. Rachel didn't so much as stir. It was strange how someone who never seemed to stop talking and seemed to be in constant motion, was now still and silent. Thomas found it disturbing. He stared at her, willing her to get better. After the doctor left, Rachel seemed to be a bit unsettled again. Thomas climbed into bed next to her and took her hand, stroking it softly.

"It'll be all right, Rachel," he murmured, trying to reassure her.

There was a knock on the door and Mrs. Brennan soon appeared. He could tell by the look on her face that she disapproved of him being in the bed with Rachel, but he didn't care.

"Lord Glenbourne, there is dinner downstairs for you," she said, going around the room, tidying up. She picked up a candy wrapper from the floor.

Thomas shook his head. "No, I'm not hungry."

The housekeeper straightened up. "When did you last eat?"

He had to think about it. "Breakfast."

"That won't do. We can't have you getting sick, as well."

"I'll be fine," he said. He didn't want to leave Rachel. He had no intention of leaving her. Certainly not for a meal.

Mrs. Brennan left the room but soon returned and said, "We've set up a table out in the hall. Your dinner is out there. Probably best not to bring food in here."

Thomas began to protest, but she held up her hand. "I'm sorry, Lord Glenbourne, but I won't take no for an answer. Now go on and get a bite to eat and a cup of tea. I'll sit with Lady Glenbourne."

Reluctantly, he stood up. The housekeeper sat in the chair next to the bed. He watched as she pulled her rosary beads from her pocket and did not take her eyes off his wife. Of everyone at the manor, the housekeeper had been most resistant to Rachel's presence. It was encouraging to Thomas that she did have a bit of a heart. Somewhere.

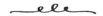

Thomas gulped down his dinner quickly, anxious to get back to Rachel.

"I'll take it from here, Mrs. Brennan," he said, returning to the room.

He removed his shoes and his tie, loosening his collar and rolling up his sleeves. Rachel's color was still ghostly pale, but she had finally fallen asleep. He did what he'd become accustomed to doing: he climbed onto the bed next to her. He lay on top of the blankets. Mrs. Brennan had an appalled look on her face. "Lord Glenbourne, I beg your pardon, but sharing a bed with the countess is most likely not a good idea."

"Mrs. Brennan, while I appreciate your concern, I plan on staying with my wife in this room, as I have every night since we were married." He had slept in this room with Rachel since the day she arrived at the manor. He certainly wasn't going to leave her now.

"This is highly unorthodox, Lord Glenbourne," the housekeeper protested.

"I'm sure it is, but she's my wife and I won't leave her," he said finally. "By all means, come in hourly to check on her, but I want to be alone with my wife. And if I need you, I will ring you."

Without another word, Mrs. Brennan exited the room.

Thomas sighed. He looked over at Rachel, who was in the middle of a deep sleep. Leaning over, he kissed her on her forehead and whispered, "Sleep well, Rachel." He lay back against his pillow, his hands clasped behind his head, staring at the ceiling. For the rest of the night, he listened to the feverish murmurs of his wife, calling for her mother, her father, her brothers. She called for everyone but him.

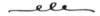

Rachel was in the deepest of sleeps. In her dream, she was with her mother and father and her brothers and the kids. They were at the cottage. It was so unbearably hot. Her parents were leaving without her. So were her brothers. She called their names over and over. She was still calling for them when she opened her eyes, expecting to be in her room at the family summer home with its paneled walls and quilted bedspread. She looked around, confused. Sunlight streamed in through the mullioned windows, casting a glow on the pink-and-ivory room. The manor. It all came back to her. She was still in Ireland. The dream had been so vibrant with color and vivid with her family that she had thought she really was back home.

She glanced over to the other side of the bed and noticed it had not been slept in. She surely could not have expected Thomas to share a bed with her when she was so ill. Still, she couldn't help but feel disappointed. Her mouth was as dry as sandpaper, and her hair felt like it needed to be washed.

Carefully, she sat up, swinging her legs over the side of the bed. There was a glass of water, untouched, on her bedside table. She brought it to her lips and realized it was flat 7-Up. She sipped it, the sweetness tasting good. But she had no sooner swallowed half a glass than her stomach rebelled, and she set the glass down and reached for the bucket, vomiting into it.

The door to her room opened, but she was too occupied retching into the bucket to notice who had entered.

"Oh Rachel!" said Thomas, coming to her and sitting on the bed beside her. "Let me hold that." In his right hand he held the bucket, while his left hand held her hair back. Gently, he brushed her hair away from the side of her face.

"Thank you," she said weakly.

When the retching stopped, Rachel sat back up. "I need to use the bathroom," she said.

"Come on, I'll take you," Thomas said.

Rachel was about to refuse him but when she stood up, her legs buckled. With his assistance, she made it to the bathroom, but when Thomas made no motion to leave, Rachel was horrified. "I'm fine. I'd like some privacy."

"You're still a little wobbly," he protested.

"I'll call you if I need you," Rachel said firmly. Even if they'd been madly in love, there were still some things she'd want to attend to privately. She took her time, washing her face and scrubbing her teeth with her toothbrush. When she exited the bathroom, Thomas stood there, waiting, hands on his hips. He was dressed in business casual: crisp shirt and dress pants.

"Rachel," Thomas said. "How are you feeling?"

"All right," she said. She made it back to the bed before collapsing. She still didn't feel right.

Thomas pulled up the blanket and tucked it around her.

"Thomas, you make a great carer," Rachel said, mustering enough strength to laugh.

He laughed too.

"Don't you have to go to work?" she asked, worried. Thomas kept a pretty tight schedule. Even though he worked from home several days a week, he was very disciplined about the structure of his day.

"I've taken the morning off."

"I'm sorry; I didn't mean to be any trouble."

He shook his head. "It's no trouble at all."

"Don't you have to go back to Dublin?" she asked, searching his face.

He shook his head. "No, I've rearranged my meetings."

"There was no need to do that," she said, worrying. The last thing she wanted to do was be a burden.

He shrugged, scratching the back of his head.

"What time is it?" she asked.

Glancing at his watch, he said, "It's almost nine."

"Nine! I thought it was six or seven." "It'd be a lot darker if it were."

There was a knock on the door, and Thomas opened it to Mrs. Brennan. She sailed past Thomas to the other side of the bed.

In a low voice, she asked, "How are you feeling today, Lady Glenbourne?"

"A little bit better," Rachel replied.

"Do you want to try some dry toast?"

Rachel shook her head. "Not yet. My stomach still isn't right."

"Best not to push it then," the housekeeper said.

"Agreed," Rachel said.

The housekeeper turned to Thomas. "Lord Glenbourne, I can look after the countess if you need to go back to work."

Thomas hesitated. "All right, then. I can catch up on some paperwork." With his hand on the doorknob, he turned to Rachel and said, "But if you need anything, will you ring me?"

She wanted to ask him to stay and sit next to her on the bed and hold her hair back like he had done several times but said nothing. She wasn't a baby and besides, surely the worst must be over. She was even thinking of showering and going downstairs.

CHAPTER FIFTEEN

T HOMAS SCURRIED AROUND THE kitchen. Rachel was coming downstairs for dinner after spending the past week recovering from that nasty virus. On the second day, she had had a setback when the vomiting increased but by evening, she was able to keep down flat Coke, and though she seemed to be taking two steps forward, one step back, she was slowly improving. To make her more comfortable, he'd had a television installed with cable in her bedroom. Luckily, her appetite had improved, as evidenced by the empty trays that had returned to the kitchen and the candy wrappers he'd noticed in her bin in the bedroom.

Grateful that she was well again, he'd been motivated to cook her a nice meal. He decided to keep it simple. And bland. He went for a traditional roast chicken with roasted potatoes and vegetables. It was about as ambitious as he'd gotten. Mrs. Shortt had smiled benevolently at him when he told her his plans, and may have even said something about love being grand.

He laid out two plates. He decided against the wine, not wanting to test Rachel's stomach.

He looked up at her and smiled as she arrived. She still looked wan. Today had been her first full day back at her desk. He hadn't counted on feeling so relieved. The manor was almost back to normal. While she'd been upstairs in bed, sick, the manor had been subdued. It had been awful. It would be awful again when she returned to the States. He pushed that as far away from his mind as he could. That first night when she was sick, she had repeatedly mentioned her mother, father, and brothers. To ask her to stay on as his wife was an imposition he was not going to ask. Even if he did love her.

Three days before Christmas, the earl left Rachel's bed early in the morning, saying something about having to clear his desk before the holiday. Rachel herself was not so inclined to get out of bed. There was still no snow, just a gray sky. And damp. She rolled over and pulled the blankets up around her shoulders. As soon he was out of the room, she scooted over to his side. It was the closest she could get to him without his knowing. His side of the bed still smelled of him and was so warm that it soon lulled her back to sleep.

Thomas crept back up the stairs. He opened the door to Rachel's room and was surprised to see that she had rolled over to his side of the bed and was sound asleep. Seeing her where he had just slept stirred something primitive in him that made him want to protect her. With tenderness, he studied her for a moment. The beautiful face and the long lashes against her cheeks. The sable-colored hair spilling over her shoulders. He'd imagined more than once touching it, running his fingers through it.

"Rachel," he whispered. "Rachel."

She stirred, opened her eyes, and jumped back to her side of the bed.

"I didn't mean to startle you," he said with a grin.

She said nothing, just blinked her eyes.

"Will you come downstairs with me?" he asked.

"Now?"

"Yes, please," he said. He extended his hand to help her out of the bed, anything just to touch her. Once she was upright, he could see the silhouette of her body through her nightgown, and he forcibly averted his eyes.

"It will only take me five minutes to get dressed," she said.

"This won't wait," he said. "Just throw on your housecoat."

She put up her hand. "I can't go anywhere until I use the bathroom."

He nodded. "Of course."

After a few minutes, she returned, brighter looking and smelling of toothpaste and face soap. She shrugged on her bathrobe, she felt around for her slippers and followed him out the door and down the stairs.

"Is everything all right?" she asked.

"Everything is fine. I have something for you," he said with a smile.

"Now I am intrigued," she said.

When they drew closer to the study, he took hold of her hand and gave it a little squeeze. She looked at him with a confused smile.

"Thomas, what are you up to?" she asked with a laugh.

The study's fireplace was ablaze. Rachel looked at it and then glanced around the room, stunned to see her parents, her brothers, and their families. Thomas watched with delight as her eyes grew wide and her hands flew to her mouth in surprise.

"Rachel!" her mother said loudly, and held out her arms for her daughter.

Rachel burst into tears. She couldn't believe it. She looked back and forth between her family and her husband, who had stood back.

There was much hugging and kissing and shouts of joy and laughter.

Thomas came forward, and Rachel introduced him to everyone in her family. Her father and brothers shook his hand, not taking their eyes off him. The earl went to shake her mother's hand, too, but Mrs. Parker pulled him into a bear hug. "We're family now, so no pretense," she said, and then she added, "Besides, we're Americans and we're huggers."

"Your husband flew us all over first class for Christmas," her brother, Robert, said, giving a nod of approval to Thomas.

"Thomas?" she turned around toward him. He had stepped further back and now stood in front of his desk. Unobtrusively, letting Rachel enjoy this reunion with her family, he was watching it all unfold with a smile on his face.

She went to him. "Thomas, you did this for me?" she asked softly, searching his face. Overcome with a mix of gratitude and love for him—the depth of which no longer surprised her—she reached out and touched the side of his face. He looked surprised. Coming to her senses, she immediately removed her hand, but he took hold of it and kissed the inside of her wrist tenderly.

For a moment, the noisy celebration of the Parker reunion was muted, and it was as if she were alone with him. For a brief moment, she thought she saw mirrored in his eyes the same things she felt for him. She could only hope.

One of her nieces, Kara, stood at her side, tugging on the sash of her robe. Rachel took the little girl's hand to be led away, but quickly turned back to Thomas, stepped up on her tiptoes, kissed him on his lips, and whispered, "Thank you." There was a look of surprise on his face, and she grinned, happy that he too, had a surprise that morning.

Her mother pulled her aside and nodded toward her bathrobe. "Is that what you're wearing to bed these days? You'll never get children dressed like that. Don't you have a peignoir?"

"Mom!" hissed Rachel. But she was distracted by her nephew and nieces and Max, who had parked himself between the two girls. He was an opportunist, that much was for sure, Rachel thought. The girls took turns feeding the wolfhound bits of pastries and scones.

Jason announced, "This dog is awesome."

Glenbourne Manor didn't know what hit it with the arrival of Rachel's mother. She had enough luggage for a grand tour of Europe, never mind visiting her daughter in Ireland for a week.

After Rachel dressed, she and Thomas took her parents on a tour of the manor. Her brothers and their wives had gone for a quick a nap to recover from the jet lag. The girls had protested loudly between yawns about going for a nap in the morning, as they wanted to play with Max, but Thomas had assured them that the dog would still be there when they came back downstairs.

"Rachel, you dark horse! You've done well for yourself," her mother said, beaming, her voice booming in the cavernous space. Her father looked around the place but withheld comment, preferring to let his wife do all the talking.

Thomas stood at her side with one eyebrow raised.

"Mrs. Parker, this way," he said.

Much to Rachel's horror, her mother performed a curtsey, bowing her head and saying to the ground with a tonal quality that put her in the running for the butler position if Percy should ever retire, "My lord."

Rachel's father shook his head and assisted his wife back up into a standing position.

Rachel shot a glance over at Thomas and saw that he had an amused expression on his face.

"Mrs. Parker, please call me Thomas," he said. "And it's not necessary to curtsey or bow; we did away with that a couple of generations ago."

"Thank God for that," Rachel's father muttered.

"Mr. and Mrs. Parker, I hope your stay at the manor will be pleasant. If there is anything I can do for you, please let me know," Thomas said.

Rachel's mother laughed. "Oh, now, none of this 'Mr. and Mrs. Parker' nonsense. It's Joyce and Glen."

"How's everyone back home?" Rachel asked. She hadn't been gone that long, but it seemed like years.

"Everyone is well," her mother said. "Your father and I went out to the site where Amy's house is being built. It's going to be wonderful. She is so grateful to you."

Rachel did not want to talk about this in front of the earl and went to change the subject, but her mother plowed on, directly to Thomas. "Did Rachel tell you what she did?"

Thomas shook his head and frowned. "No, she didn't."

"Rachel got some fantastic bonus at work, and she used it to build a new house for her friend, whose husband has suffered a traumatic brain injury. Terrible tragedy," Mrs. Parker said.

Rachel felt Thomas's eyes on her as he said, "No, she never mentioned anything about that."

"It will be an accessible house so Amy can bring Brian home," her mother said.

"That doesn't come cheap," Thomas remarked.

"No, it doesn't. Rachel used all of her bonus," her mother said.

"But not surprising," her father piped in. "Rachel always puts other people first."

"I know she does," Thomas agreed, a note of pride in his voice.

Mrs. Parker was soon distracted by the inside of the manor, as Rachel had been when she first arrived. As they followed the earl down the gallery, her mother gave her a knowing look and whispered, "Just like *Downton Abbey*."

Her mother took in everything, oohing and aahing at the portraits. "Look at all the beautiful things," she gushed.

"It must cost a fortune to run this place," Rachel's father quipped.

"He has a fortune, so it doesn't matter," Rachel's mother hissed in response.

Mrs. Parker studied the paintings of all the previous earls of Glenbourne and pronounced, "I see there are no dogs in this family." She rewarded the earl with a smile that said, "Good on you."

Rachel rubbed her hand over her face. Despite her embarrassment, she was happy to be with them again.

Her mother stopped at the painting of Thomas with the blank spot on the wall next to it. "Oh look, Glen, this is where Rachel's portrait will hang!"

Rachel glanced at the earl, who appeared to be taking everything in stride.

"When will Rachel get her portrait done?" her mother asked, always one to make sure her children weren't shortchanged.

Before the earl could answer, Rachel interrupted. "Mom, we haven't really had a chance to talk about that. Dad, you must be so wrecked from the jet lag."

"I am," her father said.

"I would suggest a little nap to get your bearings back," Rachel said.

Her mother looked at her and then deferred to the earl. "What would you suggest, my lord?"

"Please, it's Thomas. I would agree with Rachel." He looked over at his wife and smiled, and she didn't know why, but suddenly she felt warm inside.

"A little rest would do you both a world of good."

"We're not spring chickens anymore," Rachel's father said. As the tour ended, he asked, "How many acres is the estate?"

Rachel's mother perked up and paid attention.

"A little over thirty thousand acres," Thomas answered.

Mr. and Mrs. Parker went quiet. Rachel thought what a pity it was that hers was a fake marriage. The fact that Thomas had made her mother speechless made him a keeper in her eyes.

Rachel and Thomas shared a cup of coffee together in the library. Rachel's feet were practically off the ground with the arrival of her family. As glad as Thomas was that Rachel was happy, he realized yet again that despite the fact that he had fallen in love with her, he could not—would not—ask her to leave everyone and everything she loved to stay here with him. The feeling that there was such an insurmountable obstacle depressed him.

"A penny for your thoughts," Rachel said.

He laughed but felt sad. Their days together were winding down. And now that her family was there, they would have no time together alone. When their guests left after New Year's to return to New York, Rachel most likely would go with them.

They were waiting for Rachel's family to come downstairs from their naps, as Rachel was going to take them down to the village. After Christmas, Rachel planned to take them around the country to look at the different sites. The Blarney Castle over in Cork. Up to Dublin to look at the Book of Kells at Trinity College. They would take afternoon tea at the Shelbourne Hotel, and a tour of the Guinness Factory. She had asked Thomas to come along but he had refused, assuming she was only being polite. After spending three months with him, he was sure she was eager to spend time with her family. Alone.

Percy entered and said, "Jer Lynch, my lord."

Thomas and Rachel jumped up as Jer entered the room. Thomas was pleased to see that he looked spry and healthy.

"Jer! You're looking well," Rachel said, greeting him with a handshake.

"I'm feeling much better, Lady Glenbourne, thanks to you. The doctor gave me some tablets and they did the trick," he said. He paused, cap in hand, and said, "I heard you were ill as well, Lady Glenbourne. And I just wanted to make sure you were all right. I feel terrible that you may have picked something up from me.

Rachel reassured him. "I'm fine now and my virus wasn't respiratory, it was a stomach bug. So, I didn't pick it up from you."

Jer didn't look totally convinced. He twisted his cap in his hand.

"Have a seat," Thomas said. He went over to the wall and rang the bell for Mrs. Brennan to bring some tea.

Making himself comfortable on the settee across from Rachel, Jer asked her, "Are you looking forward to your first Christmas at the manor?"

Rachel beamed. "I am. Thomas has flown my family over for the holiday."

"That's nice.""What are your plans for Christmas?" Rachel asked.

"Well, I usually go to my sister's for Christmas dinner but she broke her hip last week, so I'll be home this year."Thomas watched the expression on his wife's face. He knew Jer's last statement would bother her.

"You must come here for your dinner then," Rachel said.

Jer burst out laughing. "I couldn't do that!"

"Why not?" Rachel asked, uncomprehending.

"Because it just isn't done. Me eating Christmas dinner at the manor," he said with a laugh. The expression on his face looked as if she had suggested he fly to the moon for his Christmas dinner.

"Well, maybe it's time we changed things a little bit," she said.

Jer looked to the earl helplessly as if to say, "Help me out here, and tell her how it is."

But the earl only shrugged his shoulders and grinned. "She's the boss."

CHAPTER SIXTEEN

RACHEL WALKED THE MANOR grounds with her father. The property was no less impressive now that winter had arrived, although there was still no snow. The trees on the estate were bare, and the grassy hills retained a pale shade of green. It had been a few days since they'd seen the sun.

Her father was quiet as they strolled along the asphalt drive that skirted the lawns. Massive oak trees lined the drive as well, but there was one missing in the row, victim either to the wind or to disease. Glen Parker's manner was always reserved, but today his silence seemed heavy. And ominous.

He pulled his scarf closer to his throat and shrugged his shoulders in his coat.

Rachel looked at her father sympathetically. "It's the damp, Daddy; it's a lot different than the cold."

"I'll say it is," he replied. "It's actually not that cold, but the dampness is something else."

Concerned for his comfort, she asked, "Do you want to turn back? We could go back to the manor, sit by the fire and have a cup of tea.""As wonderful as that sounds, let's walk on further."

The silence continued and Rachel tentatively asked, "Daddy, what's wrong?"

Her father rewarded her with a small chuckle. "I was going to ask you the same thing."

She frowned at him in confusion. "I don't understand."

He stopped on the path and turned to her. His warm brown eyes were kind in his face. That was one of the best of her father's many good qualities, Rachel thought. His kindness. In her opinion, there should be more people in the world like him.

"Why don't you tell dear old Dad what is really going on here?" he asked. "Because despite the fact that your mother is all caught up in this whole whirlwind romance at *Downton Abbey*, I'm not totally convinced."

Rachel bit her lip. The cold turned her nose red. She pulled a tissue from her pocket and wiped her nose.

"Is it that bad?" he asked.

She swallowed hard and looked away. "It is and it isn't."

Her father started walking again and she had no choice but to follow.

"Start at the beginning, Rachel."

She glanced around the grounds, realizing that she had grown to love the estate. The homesickness had never left her, but she was beginning to see that that had been about the people she'd left behind, not the place, like she had believed in the beginning.

As they strolled down the lane with the breeze at their backs, she poured forth her story to her father: the business project, the arranged marriage, the money for Amy and Brian, and how she would be heading home in January and looking for a divorce.

Her father paled and could not hide the look of alarm on his face. "This all started out as a work project?"

She nodded.

"And your boss went along with it?" her father asked.

Rachel nodded again and hastily added, "It was my idea to put my name forth."

"Why on earth would you do something as wild and crazy as this?" he asked. His voice was tinged with disappointment and sadness, and that felt like a crushing weight to Rachel.

"There were a few reasons actually," she started. She gathered her thoughts. "It has been pointed out to me that I'm boring, that my life lacks adventure."

"So you decided to marry a man you don't love, much less know, in order to prove otherwise?" he asked in disbelief.

"Yes, in a way," she explained. "Dad, when I'm not at work, I live like a hermit. You must have seen that."

When her father didn't say anything, Rachel continued. "I wanted to do something spontaneous and out of character. I also wanted to conquer two of the fears that have been holding me back: flying and leaving home."

"And did you? Conquer them?"

She gave a laugh. "Well, I think I've conquered my fear of leaving home."

"It still seems a bit extreme," her father said.

"I know, but I really wanted to help out Amy and Brian with the bonus that came along with it," she explained.

"That's a lot of sacrifice for someone else," he pointed out.

"But if you don't mind, then it's not a sacrifice," she replied.

"I guess not," he said with a smile.

They turned around on the path and began the long walk back to the manor.

"What is going to happen?"

Rachel shoved her gloved hands in her pockets. "Well, the agreement was only for ninety days. I'll head back home before New Year's, and then I'll get a divorce." She made it sound as simple as going to the grocery store to do the weekly shopping.

Her father sighed. "I have a feeling there is more to this than you're telling me."

Rachel bit her lip and her chin quivered. *Try to hold it together, Rachel.* But it was useless, and the tears started again.

"What is it?" Her father stopped, reached out, and laid a hand on her arm. "Has he hurt you? Has he?"

Rachel quickly shook her head. "No, no. *No.* Thomas would never hurt me," she said.

"I don't know; you're here crying, and they don't seem like tears of joy."

Rachel looked around. Everything was so quiet. The stone wall that circled the estate muted any possible noise that emanated from the village.

"Tell me, Rachel. What has upset you?" her father pleaded.

She looked at her father. "I've fallen in love with him."

"I see."

The manor came into view, and Rachel couldn't wait to get inside and park herself by a blazing fire with a hot cup of tea. A feeling of confusion washed over her. There was the simple fact that he had gone to a lot of trouble and expense to bring her family over for Christmas. When she had touched the side of his face in the study, he had kissed her wrist. Mixed signals. He *seemed* interested but it never went any further. No spoken declarations of love or even interest. Plus, he knew she'd be leaving soon, so why didn't he give her a reason to stay?

"Does he love you?" he asked.

Rachel shrugged. "I'm not sure."

"Do you plan on telling him?" her father asked.

She shook her head. "It's one thing for me to get on a plane but it's a whole different thing to muster up the courage to admit to him that I love him."

"I see." Her father sighed. He took his daughter in his arms, and she laid her head on his shoulder and cried. He patted her back. When she settled down, they resumed their walk, the manor getting closer.

As they approached the manor, Rachel decided to concentrate on the holiday and the fact that she had her family around her. Those thoughts lifted her spirits immediately. There was no sense in wondering if Thomas loved her when she had so much goodness around her.

Rachel, buoyed by the arrival of her family, became much more excited about preparing for Christmas. But it took everything she had to push out of her mind the fact that when the New Year rolled around, she would be parting ways with the earl and heading back to the States and to her old life. A life she wasn't sure she wanted anymore.

Everything had changed. But most of all, she had changed. She had not only fallen in love with Ireland—the laid-back lifestyle, the bar-none hospitality, the scenery—but most of all, Rachel had fallen in love with Thomas Yates. It was ironic how her fake husband had turned out to be everything she could want in a real one. In three months, he had turned into a husband beyond her wildest dreams. When he wasn't around, she couldn't stop thinking about him, and when she was with him, she was the happiest she'd ever been.

But it was the nights that she both looked forward to and dreaded, when they would climb under the covers together. She loved talking with him in the dark until they both fell asleep. His voice, with that Irish accent, was beautiful in the dark. She would have loved to listen to it for the rest of her life. But the desire to reach out and touch him overwhelmed her at times, and sometimes it took all her willpower not to touch him. Maybe her mother was right: maybe she should have invested in a bridal peignoir. She could now say she'd been married once, but wouldn't it be something she could treasure herself, to discover that kind of once-in-a-lifetime passion? The embers had been burning since she first laid eyes on him, and she knew that one touch from him, one caress, would set her heart and soul ablaze.

But there was one problem. Since the very first day they'd met, he'd made it clear it was strictly a business arrangement. She was simply a means to an end for him and nothing else. The fake marriage had served its purpose: the press had backed down, and most importantly, the earl's inheritance had been saved for future generations. No matter how he felt about her or what Rachel presumed he felt about her, he had yet to give her a reason to stay.

A tear slid down her cheek. She didn't want to leave but he hadn't asked her to stay. She pulled herself together and decided she'd focus on the holiday preparations, and in the meantime, she'd start thinking about packing her suitcases.

The run-up to Christmas was busy. Rachel drove her family all over the country and got in as many sights and attractions as possible. They drove south to Cork and kissed the Blarney Stone. They drove on to the port of Kinsale and walked around the colorful seaside village. Another day, they took the train up to Dublin and got on the hop-on-hop-off bus to see bits of the city center.

Back at the manor, they decorated another tree in the library. Rachel and her sisters-in-law wove a garland of pine, holly, and ivy around the grand staircase. They baked Christmas cookies with the girls. Mrs. Shortt seemed to enjoy having young children in the kitchen, as she continually fussed over the girls and let them help her. Baking, shopping, lunches in the village. Their days were busy and full.

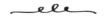

With Thomas's approval and a lot of help from her mother and the manor staff, Rachel had been working on starting a new tradition at the manor: afternoon tea for all the villagers on Christmas Day. Initially, she'd sensed skepticism from Thomas, but her enthusiasm won him over.

In bed at night, Rachel fretted whether anyone would show up to the event, but Thomas laughed and reassured her. "Don't worry, they'll come."

Christmas morning was full of excitement. Rachel's nieces and nephew were in awe of the pile of presents underneath the massive Christmas tree. Rachel had insisted that staff have the day off—it was a day for families, she'd told Thomas, and he'd relented—and for breakfast, she and Thomas cooked blueberry pancakes, sausages, rashers, and toast for her family. Later,

Thomas, Mr. Parker, and Rachel's brothers went out for a Christmas-morning stroll.

Rachel was nervous about the afternoon tea. She'd prepared for a large crowd, although she wasn't really expecting a huge turnout. After all, it was Christmas Day, and surely people would be spending it with their families. Mrs. Parker and Rachel's sisters-in-law were excited to be helping out, and between all of them, they had the grand ballroom ready to go. Rachel was surprised when Mrs. Shortt and Laura with Davey in tow arrived at the manor at half past two. Mrs. Brennan had gone on holiday to England to spend time with her sister.

"It's your day off. What are you doing here?" Rachel asked.

"We've come to give you a hand with the afternoon tea," Laura explained. Davey was positioned on her hip.

"We've had our Christmas dinner, so no worries," Mrs. Shortt said, removing her coat and hanging it up in the hall off the kitchen.

No one was more surprised than Rachel when by three in the afternoon, the grand ballroom was packed. There were lots of familiar faces: Marian, Jer, Agneta and her boyfriend, Dr. Greene, and the vicar. Even some of the staff showed up with their children, and Rachel was prepared for that, as well. She'd made up little red stockings full of chocolates and sweets for any children that might show up.

By nine, exhausted, Rachel retired to her room. She got into her pajamas and burrowed under the blankets, smiling to herself. The afternoon tea had spilled over until well past five, and with her whole family there, it was probably one of the best Christmases she'd ever had.

The connecting door opened, and Thomas entered, still dressed.

"Oh, there you are," he said with a laugh. "I've been looking all over for you."

"I was so exhausted, I decided that bed was the best plan."

"It's been a full-on day," he agreed.

"It's been a marvelous day," she said.

"It has," he said.

He seemed to hesitate, and Rachel sat back up. He took in her empty suitcases, lying open on the floor, waiting to be packed. She waited for him to say something. But he didn't.

Eventually, he came around to her side of the bed and handed her a small, wrapped gift.

"I know we didn't arrange to exchange gifts, but I'd like to give you one," he said, not looking at her but fingering the bow on the gift.

Rachel jumped out of the bed. "How truly thoughtful, Thomas!"

She accepted the gift with a smile and tore open the paper to reveal a book.

"*East of Eden* by John Steinbeck," she read. She knew before she even flipped open the pages that it was a first edition. Thomas would do nothing by half measures. She was touched. She leaned into him and gave him a kiss on the cheek. "Thank you. I love it."

When she pulled away, she saw a look in his eyes she couldn't quite identify.

Smiling, she said, "I've got a little something for you as well." From the drawer in her bedside table, she pulled out a wrapped gift for him.

She watched in excitement as he opened up his gift with an expression of curiosity. His smile grew more generous when he gazed upon the framed photo of himself as a young boy with his grandfather. Both were smiling broadly.

He looked up at her with a smile much like the one in the picture. "Where on earth did you get this?" he asked.

"I found it in the boxes of photos the staff brought down. I thought you'd like it."

He was nodding. "I do, very much. I'm going to put it on my desk."

Both were happy with their presents and finally called it a day.

The following day, St. Stephen's Day, featured a luncheon of smoked salmon, caviar, and champagne. That day flew as well, as Rachel spent it with her family and Thomas, and she couldn't remember being happier.

That night as she climbed into bed, she looked over at her suitcases. They were now half filled. Her plane ticket was laid out on the table. She'd hoped Thomas would notice, but if he did, he said nothing. And that depressed Rachel.

The truth of the matter was, she did not want to go home. But he didn't seem inclined for her to stay.

When Thomas came to bed that night, he said, "I see you've started to pack."

"Yes," she said, hopeful that this would lead to an honest conversation.

"I will have the money transferred as agreed," he said.

"Oh," was all she could manage. She rolled over, putting her back to him, and closed her eyes on the tears that filled them.

Thomas's phone rang early the morning after St. Stephen's Day. He saw it was the Dublin office, and his shoulders sagged. This would not be good. Sighing, he picked up the phone and took the call.

He found Rachel with her family in the drawing room. They were sitting around, enjoying each other's company. They were a nice family. They had gone out of their way to make him feel like he really belonged to them.

"Rachel, could I speak to you for a moment?"

She stepped outside into the gallery with him and looked at him with expectation.

He rubbed the back of neck. "The merger has fallen through."

"Oh no," she said.

"Unfortunately, I've got to go back to Dublin," he said.

"Oh," she said, disappointed. "But it's Christmas week."

He was secretly delighted at her disappointment. "It's just for a few days."

"My parents are leaving tomorrow," she said.

He nodded. "And I will say my goodbyes to them before I leave," he said. He thought of her half-packed suitcases upstairs. He'd be back before she left, and he would talk to her before she boarded that plane.

He reached out and laid his hand on her arm. "I'll be back before you go."

She nodded, but he did not miss the tears in her eyes, and that left him wondering.

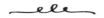

When her family left, there were tearful goodbyes at the airport. Little did they know, she'd be following them soon.

She spent the next few days packing her suitcases and boxing up anything that didn't fit into the luggage to post on home. Max followed her around and looked at her suitcases forlornly. She kept as busy as possible to distract herself from her impending departure. Thomas rang her every evening to let her know how the meetings were going and unfortunately, no progress was being made. They were back at square one. At night, she slept alone in the bed, which she hated.

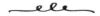

He was not going to make it back in time. He had told her that. But the more time Rachel spent thinking about it, the more painful it would be. Her flight was leaving that day, and she planned to be on it. He'd given her a lot of mixed signals. He'd always been polite, solicitous, and even had come to her defense at that party at Teddy Stabler's house. He'd even looked at her in the same way she sometimes looked at him. And there had been a couple of tender moments. But despite what she suspected—that he might feel the same way about her as she did about him—he'd said nothing. He knew when her departure date was. There was no reason for her to remain at the manor, wait for him to return, all in the hopes that he might profess his love for her. That was ridiculous. Maybe, she was just imagining things between them. She gathered her suitcases and prepared for departure with a heavy heart.

Rachel was grateful that Mrs. Maher was off, as she would ask too many questions. Questions Rachel didn't want to answer. But it was Mrs. Brennan who lobbed questions at her instead.

"When will you be returning, Lady Glenbourne?" Mrs. Brennan asked, with her eye on all of Rachel's suitcases.

"I'm not sure yet," Rachel said. She hated lying to her, but she didn't want to have to get into it.

"Seems like an awful lot of luggage for a short visit," Mrs. Brennan said, her eyes narrowing with suspicion.

"I suppose it does," Rachel said. With nothing more to say, she added, "I'd better get on the road."

CHAPTER SEVENTEEN

RACHEL FLEW HOME ON a Friday and was back to work by Monday. She'd spent the weekend moping, missing Thomas and her life at the manor. She'd been eager to get back to work, but when she walked through the double glass doors of Bixby International, she didn't feel like being there. She had lost all interest.

"Hello, stranger," Poppy said from behind the reception desk.

At work, only Mr. Bixby knew of Rachel's business arrangement with the earl. The rest of the staff were aware that she had married the earl but upon her return they said nothing about it and its obvious end.

Rachel forced a bright smile, although she felt nothing like it inside. "Hello, Poppy, how's everything?"

"Everything's fine," Poppy replied. "Boy, Rachel. You certainly surprised everybody! You marry an earl on impulse and spend three months in Ireland. Your life is more interesting than mine!"

Three months, and yet it had felt like a lifetime to Rachel. She had *lived* a lifetime in three months.

Poppy plowed on. "Was it amazing?"

Rachel gave her a smile but inside, her heart was breaking. "It was.""Do you want to meet up later for lunch? Catch up?" Poppy asked.

Rachel shook her head. "Another time."

She'd only been home a few days, but Rachel had not heard from Thomas at all, and this had disappointed her. If she had to do it all over, she might not have left so hastily. Or at least waited until he had returned. It could now be filed under "lost opportunities." Rachel kept her feelings for Thomas tucked away in her heart. When she had checked her bank account earlier, the remaining fifty percent of the bonus had been transferred to her account. Business transaction complete.

Rachel changed the subject. "What about you? How's your boyfriend?" She had asked to be polite, but she didn't think she could take any more accounts of how wonderful Poppy's life, or her boyfriend were.

"We broke up.""You did not!"

The receptionist nodded. "Actually, he broke up with me." "Why?"

"He wants to get married and settle down and have children," Poppy said, and then shook her head. "I'm not ready for that."Rachel's instinct was to jump in and offer to help. But she held back. She didn't think she had the energy to boot up her laptop, let alone solve someone else's problems. Besides, Poppy didn't seem all that upset.

Unless it was work related, Rachel was done solving other people's problems.

Thomas sat in his study, surrounded by the photos and memorabilia he had picked for the historical society. After going through boxes and boxes of photos, he'd decided to donate them, along with the camera that had belonged to his American great-grandmother, to the society. His gaze shifted from his task to the window. Looking at nothing in particular, his thoughts drifted to Rachel, as they did a thousand times a day. He put down the memorabilia, having lost interest. It had been more than a month since Rachel had left. He had not heard one word from her, nor had he been notified of any impending divorce. Her departure had left him with sorrow and disappointment that remained unabated with every passing day.

Everything was different now that she was gone. It was almost like there had been a death in the family. The manor continued in its workings, but the winsome personality it had attained with Rachel's presence had disappeared. Now it merely functioned.

That first week after she'd left had been unbearable. The manor was like a tomb. Agitated, Thomas had met with his staff and listened to their concerns and suggestions, and one of the first things he'd done was reopen the daycare. Once in a while, he heard a squeal of laughter or the collective bubble of children's chatter, and for a moment he didn't feel so morose. Mrs. Maher eyed him from time to time and then would ask if he was all right. What was he to say? That the love of his life had chosen to go home? Even Mrs. Brennan would make the odd comment, in her inimitable way, about how the place just wasn't the same without Lady Glenbourne.

He had ended up staying in Dublin for two weeks before the merger was sorted. And at the end of it, he had resigned. He no longer wanted it. Instead, he hung his shingle outside the manor for private law practice. He put an advertisement in the village paper, and it wasn't long before new business started coming in. In fact, his first client was Jer Lynch, who, at his age, thought it was time to make a will. Thomas and Mrs. Maher had already had a conversation about his need for a full-time secretary, but she was only interested in working part time, so it had been decided that she would job share. He loved working from home. What surprised him was that he didn't miss his job in Dublin at all. From time to time, he glanced at the picture of his grandfather, and he knew he was where he belonged. But a hole remained in his heart.

Glancing at his watch, he figured he should shove on, as he was meeting Sammy for lunch.

Sammy was beaming from ear to ear when he sat down at the table in the restaurant. They had agreed to meet halfway between Dublin and Glenbourne.

"Marriage seems to agree with you," Thomas noted, happy for his friend and envious at the same time. In retrospect, he could see that he had known happiness like that for three months, but that was now in the past.

Sammy clapped his hands. "Great news. Trish is expecting ."Thomas smiled. "That is wonderful news. How is she?"

Sammy laughed in good humor. "Other than being sick as a dog in the morning, she's great. Can you believe I'm going to be a father?"

The earl regarded his friend. "You're going to make a great father." At heart, Sammy was a kid. Thomas was happy for his friend but couldn't help but wonder if he himself would ever be able to share wonderful news like that. He could imagine it with Rachel but again, there was no sense in brooding on that.

As they looked over their menus, Sammy asked, "Any word from Rachel?"

Thomas shook his head.

Sammy tilted his head and seemed thoughtful, which Thomas thought was a new look for his friend. Sammy usually kept things light. He was always the one to provide levity in too, too serious situations.

"Why don't you ring her?"

Thomas immediately shook his head. "What would I say? If she felt the way I felt about her, she should have given me some indication."

"Maybe she was afraid," Sammy suggested.

"Afraid of what?"

Sammy looked exasperated. "Afraid of telling you how she felt about you?"

"Why should she be afraid? I don't bite," Thomas protested. Before he could say anything further, the server interrupted to take their orders.

"Did you ever tell her how you felt about her?" Sammy asked once the server had left.

"I didn't have to; she had to know how I felt," Thomas said.

Sammy sat back in his chair, shook his head, and sighed. "What am I going to do with you?"

For a moment, neither said anything. It was Sammy who finally spoke. "How would Rachel know how you felt about her if you didn't tell her?"

"I paid her compliments, and I cooked her dinner once a week."

"Oh, man, Tommy, you really are obtuse. Weren't those the conditions of the contract? How would she assign romantic notions to clauses?" Sammy asked.

"But I meant every compliment I gave."

Sammy shook his head. "It doesn't matter. I know how women think. I'm married to one," he said proudly.

"But I made the ultimate grand gesture: I brought her family over for Christmas."

"It's not a grand gesture if she doesn't know how you feel about her." Sammy paused. "Think about it. If she didn't have feelings for you, she would have waited until you returned from Dublin before she left. Just to tidy things up in regard to the business arrangement. She didn't ring you or leave a note because she didn't want to say goodbye."

There was silence again, and Thomas stared out the window, turning over in his mind this new idea put forth by his friend.

"What are you so afraid of?" Sammy asked.

Thomas looked back at him. "That she doesn't feel the same way."

The conversation paused as the server set their lunches down in front of them.

Sammy sighed in frustration. "Okay, let me ask you this. If you could do it over, what is the one thing you would do?"

Without hesitation, Thomas replied, "I would ask her to stay."

Sammy smiled. "It's not too late, my friend."

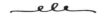

Rachel felt a flurry of emotions as she arrived at the manor. Excitement, fear, and anxiety coursed through her. Her brow was damp, her body was jittery, and her stomach did somersaults as she went up to the main doors.

She stood at the manor door and knocked.

When the stoic Percy answered, he could not hide his surprise. "Lady Glenbourne! Welcome home."

"Thank you," she said, stepping into the hall. She looked around. *I'm home.*

"Is Lord Glenbourne here?"

The butler shook his head. "No, ma'am, he's away."

Thomas wasn't there. Gah! If she wasn't so tired from jet lag or worried about what she should do next, she would have laughed.

From the corner of her eye, she caught sight of the dog, who bounded toward her, his tail wagging furiously. Rachel braced herself in anticipation as the dog lunged at her, his paws landing on her shoulders. He was as tall as she was. Her knees buckled a bit as the butler dragged the dog off of her.

Rachel laughed. "I'm happy to see you too, Max."

"Get that beast out of here!" came the voice of Mrs. Brennan.

The dog hung his head but kept his eye on Rachel. She patted his head in reassurance.

Mrs. Brennan smiled. "Lady Glenbourne, welcome home!"

Rachel was immediately escorted to Thomas's study, where tea and cakes were served. The dog collapsed in a heap at her feet.

"Will Thomas be away long?" she asked.

The housekeeper looked surprised. "Lady Glenbourne, Lord Glenbourne has gone to New York!"

It was good to be back in New York. Thomas had always loved the city, but now he was practically breathless about it, knowing that Rachel was not far from him.

A combination of emotions assailed him as he pushed through the doors of Bixby International. His stomach clenched and his hands shook. It wasn't every day that one professed one's love to a woman. He couldn't wait to see her, to look at that beautiful face again. Despite his mild anxiety, it felt like Christmas morning.

At the desk, he asked to see Rachel Parker.

The receptionist, a young woman with a lot of blonde hair and red lipstick, looked at him with a funny expression. "Your name?"

"Thomas Yates," he replied.

She picked up the phone and spoke into it. "Mr. Bixby, there's a Thomas Yates here to see Rachel Parker. What shall I tell him?" She glanced up at him and said, "Yes, I'll tell him."

Thomas frowned at her, wondering about the mystery.

The receptionist regarded him and said, "Mr. Bixby is on his way out to see you."

Thomas's stomach dropped to his knees as dread filled him. What had happened to Rachel? To *his* Rachel? Words failed him, but worst-case scenarios filled his head.

Within seconds, Mr. Bixby appeared, smiling, his hand outstretched, "Lord Glenbourne, it's good to see you again. How are you?"

"I'm well," Thomas replied, anxious to find out what had happened.

"I trust you were satisfied with our services?" Mr. Bixby pressed.

"Very much so," Thomas said.

Mr. Bixby laughed. "That Rachel is one in a million."

Thomas agreed and decided this was the segue he needed. "Actually, I thought I'd stop in and see her while I'm in town." He didn't tell him that the only reason he was in New York was to see Rachel specifically.

Mr. Bixby frowned. "Rachel no longer works here. She's resigned."

"Resigned?" Thomas repeated, wondering what had prompted that. One thing he knew for certain was that Rachel loved her job. And from personal experience was that she was a great problem solver.

Mr. Bixby nodded. "Yes, her last day was Friday. I was sorry to see her go. In fact, I offered every enticement I could think of to get her to stay."

"Where is she working now?" Thomas asked, hoping it wasn't too far away.

"She's not working anywhere. She told me she was taking six months off to travel and see the world."

Thomas's heart sank. She could be anywhere. "Do you know where she was planning on going?"

Mr. Bixby smiled. "Would you believe, she went back to Ireland?"

Thomas Yates felt as if the gods had smiled down on him. "Is that so?"

"She said there was more of the country she needed to see and that there was some unfinished business to attend to." Mr. Bixby raised an eyebrow.

Thomas couldn't stop smiling. "Very good."

"She's probably in Ireland now. Her flight left last night."

Thomas wished the man well, and as soon as he was out of the offices of Bixby International, he pulled out his phone and dialed the manor. It was Mrs. Brennan who answered.

"Lord Glenbourne, is everything all right?" she asked when she heard his voice.

"Mrs. Brennan, there's a chance that Rachel—Lady Glenbourne—" Thomas started.

The housekeeper cut him off. "She's here, Lord Glenbourne. I've been filling her up with tea and sandwiches and pastries so she won't leave."

Thomas sighed and closed his eyes. She was home. "Mrs. Brennan, please ask Lady Glenbourne to wait for me until I get there. Tell her I'm catching the next plane out and hope to be there by tomorrow." He paused and added, "Make sure she doesn't leave."

Mrs. Brennan said firmly. "She won't be leaving on my watch."

Mrs. Brennan reappeared in Thomas's study, smiling. The housekeeper had softened since Rachel had first arrived.

"That was Lord Glenbourne; he can't believe that you're here and he's over there," she said.

Rachel stood up and set her teacup down. She had consumed three cups since her arrival at the urging of the housekeeper and was fit to burst.

"Lord Glenbourne is flying home tonight, and he'll be at the manor first thing in the morning," Mrs. Brennan explained. "He's asked me to have you wait until he comes back."

"I will," Rachel said. She wasn't going to leave now. She'd wait, although her courage had dwindled. But she wasn't leaving Ireland until she said what she had to say to him: that she loved him.

"I'd better book a room in the village," she said, gathering her purse and coat.

Mrs. Brennan looked horrified. "You'll do no such thing. This is your home."

Before Rachel could protest, the housekeeper was out of the room, expecting Rachel to follow her.

As the two of them made their way to the grand staircase, Rachel looked around, happy to be back. This *was* her home.

"Mrs. Brennan, a guest room will do," Rachel said. "I don't want to inconvenience anyone."

The other woman stopped on the step above Rachel, looked back at her, and announced, "Lady Glenbourne does not sleep in a guest room in her own home." And she turned and did not say another word until they reached Rachel's room.

Rachel stepped inside, looked around, and smiled. It was just as she'd left it.

"Did Lord Glenbourne have business in New York?" she asked.

Mrs. Brennan looked at her. "I don't think so. I think he went over to see you."

"Me?" Rachel asked.

The housekeeper nodded. "He's a changed man. He quit his job and has opened up a practice here at the manor."

Rachel smiled. "That's wonderful. He'll be good at that."

"He already is," the housekeeper answered. "Do you know that he still sleeps in this bed at night?"

"He does?" Rachel asked. Something inside her lit up, and all the empty places and spaces filled with hope.

"Do you remember back when you were sick?"

Rachel nodded.

"That first night, he never left your side. In fact, he slept in the bed with you all night."

"He did?" Rachel cried. How had she not known this? Why had he never said anything? She bit her lip and thought, *Because maybe he was afraid, like I was.*

"I told him it was highly irregular, but he refused to listen," Mrs. Brennan said. "For a smart man, he sometimes doesn't have any common sense."

"Oh, Thomas has loads of common sense," Rachel protested in his defense.

Mrs. Brennan smiled. "Not where you are concerned."

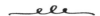

Exhausted, Rachel slipped into her old bed at the manor. It was good to be home. She soon fell into a deep, dreamless sleep. Before dawn, she felt the bed shift next to her and asked, "What time is it?"

"It's almost six," Thomas replied.

Rachel's eyes opened wide. "Thomas?"

He was at her side, pulling the blankets up around them. "My flight landed an hour early."

She blinked, looking at him, hardly believing that after all these months, he was next to her.

"I've missed you, Rachel," he whispered.

"Have you?" she asked.

She could see him nodding in the predawn light. "I have. I've been miserable since you left. You have utterly bewitched me," he said with a laugh.

With her head on her pillow, she smiled, satisfied. She liked the sound of those words. She turned on her side to face him. He reached over and laid his hand on her hip. Her heart began to beat a little faster. Her body began to relax under his light touch.

"I thought you might be interested but you never said," she whispered.

"Oh, I was definitely interested," he said. "I made a huge mistake in not asking you to stay. You had a scheduled return and I had ample opportunity."

"Why didn't you?" she asked, swallowing hard.

In the predawn light, she could see conflict contort his features.

"Because I didn't want to take you away from your family."

"Oh Thomas," she said softly, reaching out and stroking the side of his face.

His eyes were fixed on the place where his hand met her hip. His gaze drifted up her body to her eyes. "I went to New York City to tell you how I feel. I'm in love with you and want you to stay here with me at the manor. I thought it was selfish of me to want to take you away from your home."

"But my home is here, Thomas. With you," she said.

She searched his face and reached out and touched the side of his cheek. He lifted her hand, brought it to his lips, and kissed the inside of her wrist. Tenderly, he brushed the hair away from the side of her face and tucked it over her shoulder. "Rachel," he whispered.

She shifted until she faced him. His fingers made lazy circles on her shoulder, and he pushed her pajama top away and laid a kiss on her bare shoulder. As he tilted his face toward hers, Rachel's lips parted in anticipation.

And that day, Rachel Parker became the wife of Thomas Yates, the 12th Earl of Glenbourne, in every sense of the word.

EPILOGUE

"I KNEW I'D FIND you here," Thomas said, bursting through the doors of the library. His wife was curled up on a chair, a book open in her lap. "Back already?"

She closed the book and smiled at him. "Yes, the meeting for the Tidy Towns committee ended about an hour ago. Things are going well. They were asking after you." Rachel referred to Ireland's annual competition for the honor of the tidiest and prettiest town.

"I know. I'll be there for the one next month. We couldn't change the court date," he said.

Rachel nodded. "How did it go?"

Thomas smiled. "As it's his first offense, he got off with community service. He's young, and I've had a good talk with him. I told him if he kept out of trouble for one year, to come to the manor for a job."

"Very good," she said. "Sometimes, people just need second chances."

They regarded each other for a moment, each thinking about their own second chance, how they'd each taken a risk and how it had paid off.

"Come with me, Rachel," he said, taking her hand, pulling her out of her chair, and leading her out of the room.

"Thomas! What are you up to now?" she asked, laughing but following him willingly. His surprises were something else. The month before, he'd surprised her with a trip to Rome. In the spring, he'd given her the remit to redecorate the manor. Money was no object. That had become her favorite project as she tried to stay true to the heritage of the estate. Now, with his private practice, Thomas had no choice but to become involved with the villagers and their lives. And much to Rachel's delight, and as she had suspected, it was a role he'd been born to play.

They came to a halt in the gallery, where portraits of all the previous Glenbournes lined the wall. Thomas looked up at the empty space next to his portrait.

"I've arranged for a painter from Dublin to come and do your portrait," he said.

They held hands. This was Rachel's first summer in Ireland, and it had been a beautiful one. The sun was bright, and the sky was clear and everything appeared bathed in gold.

Rachel frowned. "Oh, do we have to do that right now?" she asked.

"Of course," he said, surprised.

"How long will it take?" she asked.

"A few months, but you'll sit only once a week for him initially. He'll do some sketches first."

"I don't know."

"Why are you hesitant, my love?" he asked.

She shrugged. "I don't like having my picture taken. Besides, do I really belong up there?"

The earl took umbrage at this. "Of course you do!" He stood behind her, circled his arms around her waist, and laid his head on her shoulder, kissing her neck.

Rachel laughed. "Behave yourself!"

"I can't, not when you're around," he said, kissing her neck again. He stopped and looked up at his own painting. "Look at me up there. Don't I look miserable all by myself?"

Rachel smiled.

"Once we get your picture up there, I'm going to ask the painter to repaint my mouth into a big smile. I look so grim." He grimaced.

"Oh, I don't know, I wouldn't say grim," Rachel said. "Maybe a little lonely."

Thomas pulled her hand and led her away. "Lady Glenbourne, come with me."

Giggling, she let him lead her up the grand staircase to their bedroom.

The End

ALSO BY MICHELE BROUDER

The Escape to Ireland Series
A Match Made in Ireland
Her Fake Irish Husband
Her Irish Inheritance
A Match for the Matchmaker
Home, Sweet Irish Home
An Irish Christmas

The Happy Holidays Series
A Whyte Christmas
This Christmas
A Wish for Christmas
One Kiss for Christmas
A Wedding for Christmas

The Hideaway Bay Series

Coming Home to Hideaway Bay
Meet Me at Sunrise

Lightning Source UK Ltd.
Milton Keynes UK
UKHW040703040123
414815UK00003B/257